OWNER'S MANUAL FOR THE FAMILY

HOW TO CHANGE YOUR HUSBAND

by

A FRIEND OF MEDJUGORJE

Published with permission from Saint James Publishing by

CARITAS OF BIRMINGHAM
STERRETT, ALABAMA 35147 USA

i

Published with permission from S.J.P. by Caritas of Birmingham.

Sixteenth Printing

ABOUT THE AUTHOR

The author of this book is also the author of the books Words <u>From Heaven</u>®, <u>How to Change Your Husband</u>™, <u>I See Far</u>™, <u>Look What Happened While You Were Sleeping</u>™, <u>It Ain't Gonna Happen</u>™ and other publications such as the *Words of the Harvesters* and the *Caritas of Birmingham Newsletter*. He has written more on Medjugorje than anyone in the world, producing life-changing writings and spiritual direction to countless numbers across the world, of all nationalities. He wishes to be known only as "A Friend of Medjugorje." The author is not one looking in from the outside regarding Medjugorje, but one who is close to the events - many times, right in the middle of the events about which he has written; a first-hand witness.

Originally writing to only a few individuals in 1987, readership has grown to over 250,000 in the United States, with additional readers in over one hundred thirty foreign countries, who follow the spiritual insights and direction given through these writings.

The author, when asked why he signs only as "A Friend of Medjugorje," stated:

"I have never had an ambition or desire to write. I do so only because God has shown me, through prayer, that He desires this of me. So from the beginning, when I was writing to only a few people, I prayed to God and promised I would not sign anything; that the writings would have to carry themselves and not be built on a personality. I prayed that if it was God's desire for these writings to be inspired and known, then He could do it by His Will and grace and that my will be abandoned to it.

"The Father has made these writings known and continues to spread them to the ends of the earth. These were Our Lord's last words before ascending: "Be a witness to the ends of the earth." These writings give testimony to that desire of Our Lord to be a witness with one's life. It is not important to be known. It is important to do God's Will."

For those who require "ownership" of these writings by the author in seeing his name printed on this work in order to give it more credibility, we state that we cannot reconcile the fact that these writings are producing hundreds of thousands of conversions, if not millions through grace, and are requested worldwide from every corner of the earth. The author, therefore, will not take credit for a work that, by proof of the impact these writings have to lead hearts to conversion, have been Spirit–inspired with numbers increasing yearly, sweeping as a wave across the ocean. Indeed in this case, crossing every ocean of the earth. Our Lady gave this author a direct message for him through the visionary, Marija, of Medjugorje, in which Our Lady said to him to witness not with words but through humility. It is for this reason that he wishes to remain simply "A Friend of Medjugorje."

— Caritas of Birmingham

ACKNOWLEDGEMENT

God alone deserves the credit for the publication of this book. It is from Him that the messages are allowed to be given, through Our Lady, to all of mankind. He alone deserves the praise and honor.

Special thanks and gratitude to Pat and Mary, who, through their love and generosity, provided the grant to print the first edition of this book, which, in turn, raised the funds for the next edition, thereby, perpetuating the printing of the next editions. This fifth edition is due to their initial generosity. May God reward them one hundred fold.

* * * * * * IMPORTANT * * * * * *

To understand this book fully, please read the following:

The Blessed Virgin Mary is the Mother of Jesus. She is fondly referred to as the "Blessed Mother" or "Our Lady." The Virgin Mary, "Our Lady," began appearing daily to six children in former Yugoslavia on June 24, 1981. Our Lady informed the children that She would be giving messages to the world as never before since the beginning of man, and that these were the last apparitions on earth. The tiny village of Medjugorje began to be transformed through the visits of Our Lady. The Communists, who then ruled Yugoslavia, were suspicious and persecuted the visionaries. They attempted to stop what can now be considered the most important event since the beginning of Christianity. People began to flock to the village in massive numbers. News organizations around the world began to take notice as the daily apparitions continued. *Time Magazine*, *Reader's Digest*, *Newsweek*, *Life Magazine*, *National Geographic*, The *Wall Street Journal*, ABC, NBC, CBS, BBC London and hundreds of others reported about this site and visited it. The village of Medjugorje has now been visited by over 20 million pilgrims and the fruit of the apparitions is proving it to be the center for the spiritual renewal for the entire world. In 1987, Our Lady began to give messages to the world on the 25th of each month. Through various sources, these monthly messages are spread to virtually every inhabited place on earth within hours from the moment Our Lady announces them. These messages are showing the world how to go

v

deeper into the Christian life in a world that is sinking deeper and deeper into sin and evil.

Now 30 years[*] later, all of the visionaries are adults and are married and having children. Three of the six visionaries still receive daily apparitions. The other three receive apparitions only at certain times during the year. The three who still daily see Our Lady are Vicka, Ivan, and Marija. The other three, who no longer see Her daily, but only on special occasions, are Ivanka, Mirjana, and Jakov. Throughout these writings, these visionaries will be quoted.

In January of 1987, Our Lady announced that She is bringing to the world a "plan for the salvation of mankind," especially during these turbulent times. She tells us that we cannot comprehend the greatness of <u>all</u> of our individual roles in this plan. Without a doubt, Medjugorje has changed, is continuing to change, and will forevermore change the world.

These writings are based on the messages given by the Virgin Mary in Medjugorje. When you read bold print with indented sentences in the paragraphs, these are Our Lady's words.

---

[*] This was originally written in 1996. We only updated the year in our reprinting. Often many of these writings are foreseen, even prophetic, by realizing when it was originally written – which the update could make you think it was written in hindsight rather than foresight.

TABLE OF CONTENTS

PART TWO
UNMASKING SATAN'S PLANS

FOREWORD

"It is with great excitement and joy in my heart that I recommend this book <u>strongly</u> to anyone involved in or interested in married life and family dynamics. In the twenty-three years that I now have studied and practiced marital therapy and family counseling, I have never come across anything that has spoken like this. This book reveals a view on what marriages truly are about that is hard to argue with. The reasoning is shockingly self-evident — a challenge we **must** deal with. Read this book and let it shake you, upset you, thrill you. Let it inspire you to discover a new connection between your head and your heart that will help you rise above current family troubles and immunize you against new ones. The book contains both the **dynamite** that is needed to break new rocky grounds, and the momentum needed to persevere in building a new foundation for a stable and invincibly healthy family life.

I firmly believe, that the downfall of society begins with the breakdown of the family, and the family breaks down when the marriage does. Most family counseling tries to help the parties change their patterns which is good, but change is not enough anymore. We need **transformation**, and that is exactly where this book will lead you. Don't miss the boat — time is precious!"

Dr. Peter Damgaard Hansen, PH.D.
Licensed Psychologist
Waconia, Minnesota

PART ONE

HOW TO CHANGE YOUR HUSBAND

CHAPTER ONE

WHEN A LITTLE BOY'S HEART IS KILLED

He was just 13 years old. He walked down the hall, skinny, lanky, baby-faced, with a blondish normal-looking haircut — normal in every aspect, except he had both hands bound in handcuffs. That in itself tells a sad, sad case of a little boy whose heart is grown up and hardened.

He had been given six chances to change while on juvenile probation. The county had but one choice left — to send him to Mount Megs. The juvenile probation officer [1] said, *"This is the final place for juvenile offenders when there is nothing else left."* Experience shows he will not be rehabilitated, instead he will learn how to be a better criminal, a more hardened and seasoned thief or even a killer. The rest of what is in him that is youth will be killed. He will be a hardened man in a little boy's body.

What is it that has caused this poor little boy's life to be in shreds and scarred beyond imagination? What makes the difference between him and another little boy who is the same IQ, age, class, etc., and who turns out good? What is it that can allow our children to reach the highest capability according to their abilities, personalities, IQ, etc.? What is it that will allow them to not reach their fullest potential? What makes a child whole — the most he can be? What will handicap him, even sending him down a path such as the 13-year-old? The answer to these may surprise you, and for you to benefit fully from what reading lies ahead, deep prayer from the heart is recommended. If you are reading this and are unsure about God, then talk in your heart, from your heart, to that God Whom you are unsure of or even do not believe in. Ask Him to show Himself to you. If you are Protestant, you may wish to reflect and meditate for some time, that the Holy Spirit may speak to you. If you are Catholic, go to Holy Mass and then, if possible, read this before the Blessed Sacrament. The past writings of Caritas have built one upon another. As many of you have read, the last writing was about television. Many identify that it is a problem, but no one says why it is a problem or goes to the core or to the solution. The Blessed Virgin Mary, or rather Our Lady as She is fondly called, revealed the "whys" through Her messages and what it has done to man, all of which was laid out in the June/October, 1994 Caritas newsletter. These writings again, here in this book, will, through Our Lady's messages, reveal not a surface problem but go to the core of the problem and give a solution in regard to the crisis in the family and of the youth. Many today, in all walks of life, agree the family is in trouble but offer no remedies. The core problem of what is wrong with the family will be fully addressed and specifically exposed as to a solution.

Even though the following is about changing society, the subject that will be discussed may not be what you would expect, because the secret of changing society is first and primarily in the relationship between the husband and wife. These writings are for all and they will apply and speak to you in a strong way, which will bring healing of past mistakes, happiness for the future, and improvement for society as a whole. Our Lady said on May 1, 1986:

"...Dear children, let every family be active in prayer, for I wish that the fruits in the family be seen one day..."

"I wish I had this before my divorce!"

A letter from
Sunset, Texas

...ER BONI CONSILII ORA PRO NOBIS JESUM FILIUM TUUM

A Blessed Christmas

*You will have a
special rememberance
in Holy Mass
on Christmas Day.*

While they were there, the time came for her to
have her child, and she gave birth to her firstborn
Son and she wrapped Him in swaddling clothes
and laid Him in a manger, because there was no
room for them in the inn.

Luke 2:6–7

CHAPTER TWO

WHY SOCIETY HAS BROKEN DOWN

He began backing his car out of the driveway to leave, when he felt the bump. He went limp, then began to hit his head on the steering wheel because he realized what the bump was. All too late — the terrible accident, the worst nightmare of a father — running over and killing his little child. The wife, the mother, watched the whole scene from the front porch. Gasping, seeing that her child was obviously dead, she ran. With every step her heart felt as if it were being torn out. A wife, a mother, running to a husband whose spirit had just died in this life, to a child whose spirit had just begun to live in the next life. In those first few moments, the husband's — the father's, the wife's — the mother's futures would be determined. Would the family hold together? Would there be a divorce, as many times happens in a death of a child? Would the father be able to forgive himself? Would the wife be able to forgive her husband? Would one blame the other — the mother for not checking the whereabouts of her baby — the father for not being protective enough to be ever watchful before he backed up? In this true story, the wife, the mother, in those first few seconds deter-

mined the peace or hell they would live in for the rest of their
lives. The wife, the mother, swiftly approached her dead
child, who now truly lived, and her husband, who truly wished
he could die. In that moment her first action was to run to her
husband answering his repeated cries, *"I've killed our baby!"*
by caressing him, consoling him, telling him that it was not his
fault. The wife <u>stayed</u> with him at the steering wheel.

This heroic action by the wife secured their family's future. In her decision, based on her wisdom, she immediately,
from the first instance, began the healing process for the husband and father, as well as for herself as a wife and mother.
Two years later the father was asked how he could be so radiant, happy, and content, especially after the tragedy of what
had happened. He placed it completely upon his wife, and
upon her action of coming straight to him when she could
have gone to the child. She could have said, *"Look at what
you have done." "Why didn't you look?" "Why didn't you
…?" "Why….?" "Why….?" "Why….?" "I would have gone
my whole life saying to myself, if I just would have paused. If I
just would have checked. What would have happened if …?
If….? If….?"*

This woman's desire to live first for her husband is now
her crown, in that she, as a heroine, has brought stability to
her husband and to her other children, which comes back to
her through the reward of now having a strong healthy family.

William Yates wrote of what happens when the proper order of things break down. He writes:

"Things fall apart — the center cannot hold — mere anarchy is loose upon the world." ²

<u>Everything</u> in the world has a God-ordained order. It is a sign of God, of His presence. Everything that is disorder is from satan. Disorder is a sign of satan, of his presence. God could have made the universe in chaos, yet did not, nor does it run with disorder. He made it in order. God is a God of order. Everything of order has a center, a "head." Where there is no center, there is anarchy, as Yates wrote, and *"things fall apart."*

In our solar system, there is a center, the sun, with all our planets revolving around it in fixed orbits. The sun, if it were to change just a little in any direction, would be enough to kill the earth. Our solar system, revolving around its center, the sun, at the same time also revolves with other systems in our galaxy around the galaxy's center; hundreds of thousands of them revolving in order and also revolving within themselves. Our galaxy, which would take a space craft one hundred thousand years traveling at the speed of light* to cross, also revolves with hundreds of thousands of other ga-

---

* One light-year equals about 5.9 trillion miles.

laxies, many of which are much bigger than ours — all galaxies revolving around a center in the universe. The magnitude
of this order is incomprehensible in itself, even more so when
we go back in the other direction, passing through the universe, through the galaxies' solar systems, the earth, nature,
man, to the smallest particle, an atom, and find that it too has
order. It too has electrons revolving within its universe and
different layers of smaller "planets" revolving or moving in
their designed way. It too has a center and we are still discovering more centers to the atom. It is a tiny, minute mirror of
the solar systems, galaxies, and universe, all running in order.
This thread of order you will find from the outer reaches of
the universe to the smallest particles known to man. God's
order is magnificent and where you find it disrupted, you will
find satan.

In the Garden of Eden, there was perfection. Everything changed when man fell. Therefore, all disorder can be
attributed to satan, even in nature. Our Lady said:

August 15, 1983

"...Every disorder comes from satan..."

These threads of order also apply to society. Just as
the universe is made up of smaller units called atoms, so too
society is made up of smaller units called the family. Broken

down further, between husband and wife will be found the secrets for all of society to function, just as in the atom is revealed many of the secrets of the order of the universe. If the atom's structure and order broke down and changed, so would all of the universe. Disorder would ensue, even to the outer edge of the universe. satan, with all his strength, all his intellect, all his might, wants to destroy that individual small make-up of family, the small mirror of all society, in order to bring disorder to all of society. To be specific and go deeper toward the center, satan desires to bring disorder to that particular God-ordained order between the husband and wife. Ivan, the visionary, says satan has a master intelligence. Our Lady says satan is very strong.

January 14, 1985

> **"My dear children, satan is strong. He wishes with all his strength to destroy my plans…"**

On the fourteenth anniversary, Our Lady told Ivanka at her annual apparition:

June 25, 1995

> **"satan wants to destroy the family. The family is in crisis. Pray."**

Within the unit of the family, the children's lives revolve around the parents, and to break it down further toward
the **core**, the center is the husband and wife's relationship; i.e.
the relationship to each other, their treatment of each other,
with the husband guiding and the wife following. He is the
center; he protecting; she nurturing; he fathering; she mother-
ing — on and on. If based on God's precepts and love, this
relationship contains every lesson, every teaching their children will need to be whole and to make up society. Society's
cure lies within the relationship and attitude of the husband
and wife toward each other. It is why satan wants with all his
might to destroy the sacramental union. Ivan, when asked
about satan being the cause of divorce answered:

> *"Of course divorce is the product of sin. Sin is*
> *the result of strong temptation. Sin is the result*
> *of weakness. At least one party in a marriage has*
> *to sin to **destroy a sacramental union.** Whenev-*
> *er there is sin, there is satan. How does satan be-*
> *come involved in a marriage? Many ways. One*
> *of his favorite ploys is to divide husband and*
> *wife, then go after the children one by one."* [3]

To split the atom is to cause a nuclear explosion —
chaos. To split a husband and wife is to cause a societal explosion — chaos. These writings are about that order through
which, if followed, divine order will come and marriages, fam-

ilies, society, and the world will heal. satan has minimized, disguised, and even killed this order of structure in the family. By doing so he attacked the authority of God the Father, which will later be shown in these writings. It has happened through the "woman's" disobedience and the "man's" weakness to stand up and take charge, just as in the Garden of Eden, when Adam did not stand up to Eve in her disobedience, but rather followed her. satan in his cunning used his best trick in the Garden of Eden. The plan by which he attacked man successfully the first time, he has carried out now in the present age.

*"Although I did not live this (submission) through the early years of my marriage, bringing great harm to the lives of myself and family, through God's grace, I am now living this request — 'command' — of the Lord. And I am reaping **great** benefits — peace in my heart and soul, the love of my husband, and peace and harmony in our home and lives."*

A letter from
Bismarck, North Dakota

CHAPTER THREE

REPAIRING THE BREAKDOWN
OF SOCIETY

Recently at a youth retreat, the speaker was talking to boys and girls ranging in ages 14 to 18 years old. He said, *"There is an order to everything in which it is to function properly. The family is no different. Husband and wife are not equal in authority in the family. The man is in charge, the head. The wife is subject to him."* Immediately he noticed two different reactions from the youth. Before him, several young men nodded their heads in agreement and the young women smirked in disagreement.

Several months ago during Sunday Mass, the pastor read the Gospel which contained the following verse:

Eph. 5:22

> **"Wives should be submissive to their husbands as if to the Lord, because the husband is head of his wife, just as Christ is head of His body, the Church, as well as its Savior. As the**

Church submits to Christ, so wives should submit to their husbands in everything."

"Husbands love your wives as Christ loved the Church. He gave Himself up for her to make her holy, purifying her in the bath of water by the power of the word..." [4]

The homily began with the priest speaking about loving the wife and everything related to it, but throughout the homily he completely ignored any hint of wives' submission to husbands.

In truth, the subject of submission has been largely ignored by a large number of priests, counselors, directors, and others for quite some time. This is the case with most who are in a position of authority to speak about it. It is as if a taboo is placed upon this subject which is repeatedly discussed in the Gospels with such clarity and strength that its meaning is undeniable. And yet it is increasingly squashed and silenced, as was the case with the priest in the previous paragraph. In textbooks, the media, society, even religious and diocesan newspapers and from the pulpit itself, from a large percentage of both priests and bishops, you will find many thoughts reversing or neutralizing this order of the Scripture, that wives have a freedom to do whatever they want or at the most, be only somewhat obedient; that the husband's authority is not different from the wife's, that everything is equal, that we should compromise. Those who know this thinking is not right are labeled sexist and are muted or silenced out of fear that they will be viewed as unfair.

In any topic of conversation when you hear discussed, *"Wives submit to your husbands,"* the response is, *"Yes, but husbands love your wives."* This, in turn, leads to a discussion of only this aspect — love your wife — and it usually dominates the conversation, homily, text, etc., just as the example of the priest already given. There exists a clear imbalance in the attention given this subject; **therefore, what is rarely mentioned will be given the primary attention in what follows. It is the most important spiritual direction Caritas of Birmingham** * **has ever printed, because if it is followed, it <u>will</u> work, since it is based on solid Scripture, backed with Our Lady's messages and the lives of the saints.**

---

* Caritas is a mission whose purpose is to inform others of the Virgin Mary's messages, and what they mean for the world.

"I am a married professional woman with a family of my own. I can remember saying to a colleague that what I needed most at home was a 'wife to take care of me!' I said that I needed to work to help pay the bills, but it was because I wanted a bigger house and nicer things than I grew up with.

"In applying the truth from your book to events in the world today, what you have written really does make sense. I just finished reading a book called <u>How to Listen to God</u> by Charles Stanley. In it Rev. Stanley says we know it is God speaking to us if it is consistent with the Word of God, conflicts with human wisdom, clashes with fleshly nature, challenges us to faith, and calls us to courageous acts. The words in your book meet all five requirements.

"You are right. I believe that the evils troubling our nation today stem from the rebellion of women against God's will. My parents also insisted on my higher education because they thought a woman must be able to take care of herself in this society today, in case her husband divorces her. I still believe that a woman needs to be educated today to be a good wife and mother, but no one teaches the things she really needs to know to be successful at it."

A letter from
Shepherdsville, Kentucky

CHAPTER FOUR

ARE YOU NARROW OR BROAD-MINDED ABOUT SUBMISSION?

When you look at a deep topic it is necessary to view it from every angle, every "point of view." If you were to view a tree in a field from a short distance away, then walk, circling the tree, you would see a different view at each step. A little more would come into view with each step. If you walked only half way around, your "point of view" would be limited only to those points from which you viewed the tree. The person who viewed the tree, making a complete circle, is able to have a better perspective and understanding, a broader view of the entire make-up of the tree. The person who views it from only one side is more narrow in his "point of view," because he sees only half of the points compared to the ones who made the full circle. It is just a simple tree. Yet, to see it completely one must see it at every angle. As the tree is the center of the circle in the above example, these writings will make a full circle around a single topic, a single point, that being the Bible passage: *"Wives be subject to your husbands."* While only six words, it must be looked at from every point of view. The meaning of these words are so profound and have such impact on the world that it was difficult to contain the entire subject in so short a writing. However, enough has been written in the following pages to go full circle around most every point of view concerning this subject. This is necessary in order to illustrate that our understanding of this verse is far from being narrow. Rather, those individuals who presently object, either fully or partially, to this Bible verse are most likely narrow in their view of it, but it is our hope that the re-presentation of the Scriptures concerning this verse will bring about a broader understanding of it. Therefore, as you "walk around" this verse, viewing it from every angle, you will examine many subjects, read many stories, contemplate many quotations all the time, coming back to the center point being examined, which is the verse, ***"Wives be subject to your husbands."*** Its purpose is not to drill into your head this verse, but to open your heart, your mind, your spirit to a broader understanding and joy of what this verse contains, rather than the narrow-mindedness which prevails today. This narrow-mindedness has mislead many, even Christian women, to believe that subjection to male authority leads to the degradation of women, turning them into second-class citizens, when, in fact, it is a lie and the verse actually is the opposite, in that it leads to freedom and the blossoming of womanhood. To live this verse is to elevate women to a much higher status, a status which does not exist today, mainly because of the rejection of this verse in the present lives of wives and mothers, as well as all of society.

It is important to note that women, who are not loved by their husbands, are not free to be disobedient, and men, who are not obeyed by their wives, are not free to stop loving them.

Our Lady is coming to give us an example, a witness of how to live our lives, a witness that She wants us to follow. She wants us to fulfill "our roles" in the same way She did, when She was a wife and mother on earth. These writings will focus on Our Lady's example to us; what She is leading us to specifically in regard to submission to God the Father and to the order that He established for families to live in peace. The living of Our Lady's messages, together with the beautiful fruit it brings, supports and brings to further light the Holy Scripture.

The first thing to realize when we hear, *"Wives be subject to your husbands,"* is that the other side of the coin is not *"husbands love your wives."* Rather, it is, *"Husbands be subject to the Father in Heaven."* The other side of the coin of, *"Husbands love your wives,"* is *"Wives love your husbands."* To flip these as opposing statements is a gross error which has prevailed in most areas of thought today. It is not intended as, *"Wives be subject to your husband,"* vs. *"Husbands love your wives.*" Rather, wives be subject to your husbands, husbands be subject to the Father, then the both of you will be in God's will and in peace, which will bring about the fruit of real love of husbands loving your wives and wives loving your husbands, a union of the two statements — rather than a response to counter someone who mentions the first part or second part of this verse.

These few words — *"Wives be subject to your husbands"* — if lived, will bring about divine order and will be the beginning answer for all of society's ills. The fact that this order hardly exists today, or is weakened to such a degree that a husband's guidance is watered down to almost nothing, is reflective of a society gone mad. **God, as a Father, does not leave man, who is the first reflection of God the Father on earth, without the divine prompting necessary to lead and guide his family.**

Is it important for us to understand we have roles which are ordained by God? Yes, because a wife's place is to bring peace to her home. A husband's role is to maintain the peace. If this is not understood properly, it leaves a lot of room for satan to enter and cause great disruption and chaos in the home.

Pope Pius XI, in an encyclical to all bishops of the world in 1930, wrote:

"For if the man is head, the woman is the heart,
and as he occupies the chief place in ruling, so
she may and ought to claim for herself the chief
place in love." [5]

This action of husband leading, guiding, and the wife obeying, following, will teach children how to obey a police officer, teacher, and those in authority later. One action of rebellion by the wife toward the husband can damage a child's whole respect for authority with police, teachers, church, or anyone who is in a position of authority. A wife telling the husband to "shut up" will definitely lead to the children telling the mother herself to shut up, as well as them saying it to the father. Authority is not always right, perfect, or on target, but we are not excused from having deep respect for that authority simply because we do not see eye to eye or understand it or agree with it. To lack proper respect is to pull apart the central authority. The center and what surrounds it will not be able to hold together and keep order which, in turn, undermines those who are most in need of its protection and who are the ones who destroy the order to start with by their disrespect. Once authority is usurped, it is lost and almost impossible to regain. When the time arises for those who rebelled against it to seek out its protection, it is not possible because it is no longer there. The French Revolution gives an example of this entire scenario, and the results were disastrous, as the rebellion was waged against God's authority. The authority, at the time, in France was not perfect but afforded people law and order. Rebellion against the king eventually led to rebellion against God and His authority. This authority was disrupted by disrespect and rebellion which led to total anarchy, in which tens of thousands were massacred, as well as virtually <u>all those who started the anarchy to begin with</u>. As the usurpation of authority led to rebellion against God Himself, it birthed <u>masonry</u> and <u>liberalism</u>. These movements are the children of the French Revolution. A wife's rebellion and disrespect toward her husband will do the same in the family, and when she calls for the husband's help to control the children, he will not be able to help, for his authority was damaged or even killed by the wife. Both of them will lose control. Just as when things got out of hand in France, and suddenly when many wanted the king to step in to bring order, he could not, having been so severely undermined. While the king was not perfect and had his share of faults, living under his command was like living in the Garden of Eden compared to what the French were to suffer in the next decades to come. France, to this day, is living a revolution against God. Mothers must be aware of the importance of their words and actions, because they have the power to determine future peace or anarchy. Wives may think they do none of these things—rebellion, usurping of authority, disrespect of husband, etc.—yet the small, minor instances of disrespect have a

major impact on their children, as well as their husbands, as
the following shows:

> *"One Christian mother tells of a normal morning*
> *when the family had finished eating breakfast,*
> *and she was cleaning up the dishes as usual. Her*
> *little daughter was helping her put the dishes in*
> *the dishwasher, when suddenly she looked up at*
> *her mother and asked so innocently, 'Mommy,*
> *why do you always make Daddy so unhappy be-*
> *fore he leaves for work?' The mother, taken ab-*
> *ack by such a question, asked her young daugh-*
> *ter what she meant. She replied with total hones-*
> *ty, as only a young child expresses, 'Well, what-*
> *ever Daddy says, you always tell him he doesn't*
> *know what he's talking about. And then Daddy*
> *stops talking and looks real sad.'"* [6]

It is important to note that if the wives spoke in depth
to their husbands in this present time, they would be surprised
to find out how often they are doing this to their husbands.
Many men today truly want to execute their authority in their
families and in a just way, but are blocked by their wives. The
father, hopefully following God's precepts, if allowed to
guide, will teach children once they themselves are in authority how to exercise it. Peace will flow from the mother, maintained by the father. It is the heavier responsibility of the

mother to change society now by becoming submissive. Wives are not excused if husbands are not submissive to the Father. Scripture says husbands will be won over by the wives' holiness and submission.

1 Peter 3:1–2

> *"Likewise you wives, be submissive to your husbands, so that some, though they do not obey the word, may be won <u>without a word</u> by the behavior of their wives, when they see your reverent and chaste behavior."*

The cure of society will begin there with the father being the center, the wife around him, and the children around them. It is the atom, the make up of how society is to function, all obedient to religious, civil, and government authority. As the atom mirrors the entire structure and workings of the universe, so too in the relationship of the husband and wife, the family mirrors and reflects society as a whole and how it is to work. Many now recognize that our future depends on the family. Both religious and non-religious are all beginning to see this fact. However, no one is going to the core and telling us what the family needs to change to bring it back to health. Even religious do not go deeply enough to find the problem and offer a remedy. A quote in a magazine about the restoration of the family is a general picture of virtually all of those who recognize that the problem in the world is the family, but do not go deeper to find the true problem and the true remedy. The quote:

> *"...the family is the core of our nation. We have fought to stabilize the family through information, prayer, public policies. Our most recent lobby..."* [7]

To what will it avail us to lobby to change laws if the family does not know how to function? Passing laws will not damage satan's gains in destroying the intimate working structure of the family. We say it is divorce, incompatibility, etc. but why do we have this anarchy? Why can't the center hold? Why is it falling apart as Yates writes? The father has been usurped. His role diminished. The most he has, if even that is offered, is his being equal in authority with the wife. He is no longer the center, just as God the Father's authority is no longer the center of society, and this is the reason it spins out of control. One wife wrote she had been praying for her husband's conversion for years. He was a pagan in most ways. He recently converted and she was amazed that what took her years to gain in the spiritual life, he suddenly knew and was able to guide her in a superior way. We must ask ourselves, why not? Why would God not give the leadership and guiding ability to man since He ordained it to be so from the beginning? It is not to say women's prayers are not <u>equally</u>

heard by God. They are! It is not to say she will not receive answers and inspirations to her prayers equally with any man. But the submission of those inspirations are to be in union with whatever state they both are in, just as a holy person under spiritual direction submits and is in union directly with that director. If a wife says her inspiration is telling her to do something which contradicts the husband, it is the husband who must be obeyed unless, of course, it is a sin.

The book **Me? Obey Him?**, by Elizabeth Rice Handford, states:

> *"Suppose a woman feels God is leading her definitely opposite to what her husband insists she do. It's something that is not addressed in the Scriptures, it can't be clearly found in the moral law of God, but she feels very strongly that God wants her to act contrary to what her husband demands. Whom should she obey? The <u>Scripture</u> says a woman must ignore her 'feelings' about the will of God and do what the husband wants her to do 'as if' God had spoken audibly from Heaven!*

> *"It's hard to believe that the man you are married to, loveable and wonderful as he sometimes is, often grumpy and temperamental, it's hard to be-*

lieve that man could be the actual voice of God in your life, but Numbers Chapter 30, verses 6– 16 states it. This passage teaches two major truths: one, that a husband is given the right by God to prevent his wife from taking a spiritual step she feels led to take; and two, that if he does, God holds him accountable — 'He shall bear her iniquity.'

"Here is a good woman who feels a burden to do a certain thing for God. She makes a vow to do so. In obedience to God's Word, she asks her husband's permission to do it. If her husband 'disallows' it, if he will not permit her to do it, then God says she is free of her vow. Her husband is the one who will stand accountable to God for it. If it turns out that his decision is wrong, then he is the one who will bear the blame.

"Why did God make this rule? Because it is a burden too heavy for a woman to bear, if she is required to assess every decision of her husband's to ascertain if it is really right or wrong. If she is forced to determine what is right, and act accordingly, then her behavior cannot be called obedience. She is making the final decision about what she will or will not do. God never in-

> *tended for a woman to have to be accountable to*
> *Him for the rights or wrongs of her husband's*
> *decisions. If she does right consistently, then*
> *God will protect her from having to do some-*
> *thing morally and irretrievably wrong."* [8]

Elizabeth Rice Handford writes later:

> *"Does God really mean it when He commands a*
> *wife to be in subjection to her husband? Without*
> *a doubt! It is a positive and direct command*
> *God expects to be obeyed, in faith, knowing and*
> *doing the will of God regardless of the conse-*
> *quences.*
>
> *"What if my husband won't actually forbid me*
> *to do something but says he'd rather I didn't?*
>
> **"Remember we are talking about a <u>heart attitude</u>**
> **of submission, not a letter-of-the law obedience.**
> **So you ought not to disobey your husband just**
> **because he forgot to say the magic words, 'I for-**
> **bid it.' You won't be looking for loopholes; you**
> **will be sincerely trying to please him."** [9]

We ended the previous chapter by writing it will work, and the following chapters will <u>show</u> you it works.

IT WORKS

*He rattles his glass; she jumps
up fast and pours him a glass
of tea.
Deep in her heart she believes
that's the way it should be.
And I've seen my dad get figh-
tin' mad over one little four-
letter word.
He'll tell you fast, you don't
talk like that around her.*

*We may not see it the way
they see it.
We may not do it the way they
do it.
She lives her life for him, and
he'd gladly die for her.
And even in this modern age,
it works.*

*Though he's been down on his
back, he still jumps out of
that sack every morning at
5:00 am. Having her home
with the kids has been worth it
to him.
And she takes pride in being
his wife and making their
house a home.*

*And sometimes she wishes the
world would just leave them
alone.*

*We may not see it the way
they see it.
We may not do it the way they
do it.
She lives her life for him,
and he'd gladly die for her.
And even in this modern age,
it works.*

*If the Good Lord's willing,
there will come a day when
our children will say:*

*We may not see it the way
they see it.
We may not do it the way they
do it.
She lives her life for him.
He'd gladly die for her.
And even in this modern age,
it works.*

Sung by the country music group
"Alabama."
© used with permission

34

CHAPTER FIVE

WOMEN WHO SUBMIT TO THEIR HUSBANDS ARE NOT DOORMATS BUT REFLECTIONS OF MARY

Our Lady is coming to change society. She is not supplanting God the Father's role. All Her actions are one of total submission to the Father. Is Our Lady not the Mother of Jesus? Did not the Holy Spirit conceive in Her? Do we not say She is the spouse of the Holy Spirit, Jesus being Her Son — Their Son? Does this not then mirror the divine order that all husbands and wives should reflect? Was there even one occasion when Our Lady was disobedient to the inspirations of Her Spouse, the Holy Spirit, especially when it was excruciatingly painful to do so? It is through Mary that the world is being taught to love, honor, respect and obey God the Father, and by this means the world will be saved. By following the example of Our Lady, wives and mothers are to re-establish fatherhood by honoring and respecting their husbands. They are to parallel what Our Lady is doing on a large scale, leading all of mankind back to reverence towards God, by re-establishing reverence for their husbands in their own homes. Men will not be able to force it without the wives submitting to their fatherhood. It is first upon the mothers to do so. It is not at all difficult to find that Our Lady's messages contain within them the underlying theme of obedience to God's structure of the family. Her every message is "family," as She begins every message with **"Dear Children."** As a wife and mother, She supports God the Father's role, thereby teaching all husbands and wives how they are to be as fathers and mothers. Our Lady's messages are more about support for motherhood and contain more about it than any other subject which She speaks of. Her messages, Her motherhood, Her every action guides Her children towards respect for God the Father in Heaven. Our Lady's response and submission to God the Father, and the Father's reaction and love back to Mary, gives the example for motherhood and fatherhood on earth. The wife's response to her husband in honoring and obeying him, and the husband's response back to his wife, in loving and taking care of her actually parallels the love between God and Our Lady.

Those who are mothers give their blessing upon their children as a mother when they support and obey the husband and father. The mother's blessing through obedience makes it so that fathers, in turn, will have a strong desire to give abundant support to provide as best they can for the <u>daily life</u> of those who depend on them.

Our Lady reflects this so perfectly in Her message of
July 25, 1992:

> **"...I bless you with my Motherly Blessing, <u>so</u>
> <u>that</u> the Lord may bestow you with the abun-
> dance of His grace for your daily life..."**

This message shows Our Lady and Jesus blessing, but
also here is a message from Heaven clearly showing that a
husband, which Scripture says is the Lord of his wife, depends
on the wife and mother's blessing and cooperation in order to
be the most capable provider he can be. A wife's submission
to her husband will affect even the material blessings as well
as peace in the family, as shown and paralleled in the above
message. Our Lady amazingly shows the crisis of the present
rebellion of women, which the young girls at the retreat
smirked at, while the young men agreed with it. In Medjugorje, during one apparition, Our Lady did something She
had never done before. She singled out all mothers for a special blessing. On December 19, 1985, Our Lady said:

> **"...I wish in a special way on Christmas Day to
> give mothers my own Special Motherly Bless-
> ing..."**

Even more remarkably, She then emphasized that this is just
for wives and mothers by saying:

"...and Jesus will bless the rest with His own blessing..."

The above message of Our Lady makes a profound statement. Women hold a profound power, a power and strength to run the world, and yet society has placed them in a position of giving it up. In 1872, a woman marched in before the officials and demanded to vote. Susan B. Anthony felt that this was so important that she went all over the United States, speaking to other women, saying that women were being treated as second class; that it was time for all women to be treated the same as men, etc. The presenting of this example is not to say women shouldn't be allowed to vote. Rather, it is to show the trading of the direction in which the power of women began to fall. In all of this event, few have the wisdom to see what really took place with this new freedom for women and with thousands of other incidences which began to raise up, or perhaps rather bring down, the dignity of women. Wifehood, at that time, was still held in great esteem, with great respect. Old newspapers of historical Williamsburg reflect the high esteem of homemakers and wifehood. Even going back to ancient Israel, motherhood was held in the greatest honor, a throne. *"She who rocks the cradle rules the world."* Indeed it was true. The influence of a mother who had six children, say, three boys and three girls, who devoted her all to her husband and children, who raised them with her influence being so strong in union with her husband's, was literally stamped in them for the rest of their lives. The woman, who "mothered" in this way, would have voted three times every time her boys voted when they grew up. Her girls, having, say, three boys each, gave her another nine votes, totaling twelve more votes with grandchildren, etc. This influence of motherhood, though veiled, is immensely powerful.

When women began to seek individual accomplishments, desires for themselves, their own space, they actually began to lose power. A mother sitting in a board room of a company today has far less impact than the mother who raises five boys to do the same. These five boys once raised will then sit in board rooms or other positions and cast their decisions daily through their entire life, which would be influenced by their mother, thereby making the mother have far more reaching influence than if she sat in the boardroom herself. We say, **"But women can do as much as men! They can be fighter pilots, manage offices, run corporations, etc."** No one is arguing that, because it is true!! Why should that not be so? A woman, who was ordained by God to handle motherhood, certainly could handle second rate jobs, such as being the chairman of the board of a corporation. A woman has tremendous energy and capability to be a mother, which God has granted to **her,** not to man. **A woman is over qualified to be the head of a college or fly an F-14 high tech fighter jet. Taking care of three children under five, managing a household, and taking care of a husband takes far more capability and superior wisdom and intelligence than any job the world**

offers. God offers women Motherhood.[*] **The sacrifices it requires will be the jewels she will wear in her crown to come,
earned through years of sacrificial love.** And when her hair will
begin to gray, full and content will be her days, making all other
jobs other career women choose as nothing, their harvest empty.
Many women with good intentions are deceived into working
outside the context of the family, as the following letter shows:

> *"It is true; many women are working for selfish
> reasons. But, there are many who are not con-
> scious that this is wrong because society has led
> everyone into this way of thinking. I was encour-
> aged to get a college education by both of my par-
> ents who were holy parents and wonderful wit-
> nesses. I went that route to please them and com-
> pleted my degree. But now I recognize that we
> have again been duped by satan, thinking we were
> doing something good and noble when we were ac-
> tually weakening the family's foundation."*

There is no argument being made that women shouldn't be
educated. The point being made here is "<u>what</u>" women are
being educated about. The Bible tells us in Titus 2:3:

---

[*] Of course God offers women the possibility of serving Him as a religious. This too is a
form of motherhood, as women choose this life to help birth conversions, or birth love in
little hearts as a teacher, etc., through their vocation.

"Similarly the older women must behave in ways that befit those who belong to God. They must not be slanderers, gossips, or slaves to drink. By their good example, they must 'teach' the younger women to love their husbands and children, to be sensible, chaste, busy at home, kindly, submissive to their husbands. Thus the Word of God will not fall into disrepute."

Does not "logic" speak clearly that this is no longer taught to women by older women, and that society has fallen in disrepute? Is God's word here to be ignored or rationalized away? Of the six attributes the Bible says to teach young women, which of these are taught in college? In fact college teaches the opposite:

BIBLE	**COLLEGE**
1. Love your husband/children	Love yourself first
2. sensible	intellectualism
3. chaste	loose
4. busy at home	busy at career opportunities
5. kindly	demanding
6. submissive to their husbands	"No man tells me what to do"

Can there be any wonder why the Word of God has fallen in disrepute when that is exactly what it says will happen?!

Other women, not going the education route, are still taking the easy way out, taking jobs outside of the home all for self, materialism, and yes, hidden laziness, because it is easier than staying home and raising their own children. This has actually led to the loss of motherly skills. Father Paul Wickens, in his pamphlet "Handbook For Parents," states:

> *"Many career women — capable of running large offices with efficiency and skill — are incapable of managing a two-year-old."* [10]

This is scandalous, but Pope Pius XI, in his encyclical goes further, saying this kind of emancipation of women is a crime:

> *"....(If) the woman is to be freed at her good pleasure from the burdensome duties properly belonging to a wife, a companion, and mother (we have already said this is not an emancipation but a crime), inasmuch as the wife being freed from the cares of children and family should to the neglect of these be able to follow her own bent and devote herself to business and even public affairs where-*

by the woman even without the knowledge and against the wish of her husband may be at liberty to conduct and administer her own affairs, giving her attention chiefly to these rather than to children, husband, and family.

"This, however, is not the true emancipation nor that rational and exalted liberty which belongs to the noble office of a Christian woman and wife. It is rather the debasing of womanly character and the dignity of motherhood and indeed of the whole family. As a result, the husband suffers the loss of his wife, the children of their mother, and the home and the whole family of an ever watchful guardian. More than this, this false liberty and unnatural equality with her husband is to the detriment of the woman herself, for if the woman descends from her truly regal throne to which she has been raised within the walls of the home by means of the Gospel, she will soon be reduced to the old state of slavery. If not in appearance, certainly in reality and become as amongst the pagans, the mere instrument of man." [11]

How true it is that women are used today by the media, the job market, etc. as instruments, much because of their own rebellion in not wanting to follow man.

"I yielded to my husband, certainly, when and if it suited me! If it didn't so suit me, well... I choked his every effort to assume his rightful leadership in our home and I did many things which undermined and weakened his authority.

"Its ('How to Change Your Husband') message was the very submission I had so been avoiding and yet yearning for all at once. Thanks, Caritas, for having the strength to speak the truth, even when it's unpopular."

> *A letter from*
> *Havertown, Pennsylvania*

CHAPTER SIX

HUSBANDS/WIVES
EQUAL WORTH — YES!
EQUAL DIGNITY — YES!
EQUAL AUTHORITY — NO!

Cardinal Bernard Griffin warned mothers of his day:

"Do not allow anyone to deprive you of the care of your children. Do not allow men to encourage you to deprive yourselves of the greatest privileges you have as mothers to train the body and soul of your child. <u>Outside the home you become a worker, a hand, a cog in the machine. In a factory you will be engaged in dealing with lifeless material.</u>

"In the home, as a mother, you will be fashioning the greatest object of God's creation. You can teach your child to love and honor God and by so doing to love and honor other people. It is your greatest contribution to the moral reconstruction of this country." [12]

The above situations mostly lie within women's decisions in varying degrees to abort motherhood and claim equality in authority with man. Men and women do have equality and the same rights which belong to the dignity of the human soul, and it is properly so ordained by God. These are God-given and <u>equality before God of the soul must be recognized.</u> A woman is equal in worth with man. She is equal in dignity, and even entitled to higher dignity than man. She is not, however, equal in authority with man. Still this does not lower her worth, rather as a person, she is more valued and her dignity rises. The marriage itself holds certain obligations in equality between both the man and woman such as faithfulness, love, consideration, etc. But there is a certain inequality for the good of the family in regard to its function, structure, and stability. Pope Pius XI writes:

> *"...in other things, there must be a certain inequality and due accommodation, which is demanded by the good of the family and the right ordering and unity and stability of home life."* [13]

The "equality" thinking which prevails in marriage today in which Pope Pius calls the promoters of such thinking "false teacher," [14] is the basis for most problems in marriages today. Even if hidden by various other issues which might be a problem in marriage, such as money, T.V., pleasures, drinking, etc., once this error is recognized and corrected, the issues begin to solve themselves. By exposing the root of the problem and conforming to the Scriptures through obedience and submission, all issues which divide the husband and wife will be resolved. The husband is to look to God, the wife to the husband. It does not mean he is not to listen to his wife's wisdom and allow "reason" to prevail, but in all his decisions he must be accountable to God and be in union with the will of God the Father. When the wife's requests to the husband are not in conflict with God's direction and guidance to him (the husband), then he should compassionately grant to her those needs if he is able. However, many men who know what to do allow their passions to "compromise" their direction. Eventually, fearing his own passions* and being worn down by them, the husband gives in when a wife wants to go in the wrong direction, granting her freedom to do what she wants when it is opposed to his direction. Ivan, the visionary of Medjugorje, who still sees and speaks to Our Lady daily said in August, 1994:

> *"I don't have anything against women. Women are a touch of God. But some of them, especially in other countries such as the United States, make many problems for their husbands and for their*

---

* To be specific, fearing the loss of temporary or long-time conjugal relations with his wife, he, for the sake of his passions and desires, compromises his direction rather than risking the loss of intimacy, which some wives threaten if things do not go as they want.

marriage. This is because they want '<u>things</u>.' Be-
cause they want things (or their way) and cannot
have them, they (the wives) then use force, for in-
stance, refuse intimacies with their husbands, etc.
Husbands then become tired of them, tired of
everything and give in. The wife, through this,
takes away his freedom (his rights as a husband
and she begins to control him through these
means). He is no longer free. He is like a slave
to her and that leads to divorce." [15]

After Adam and Eve's fall, God ordained that wom-
en's urges (wants) are to be for the husband:

Genesis 3:16

"Yet your urge shall be for your husband."

If a woman fulfills God's command, she will be content
and at peace. If not, she will never be satisfied with herself. It
is, therefore, God who ordained that a wife's wants should be
the wants of her husband and not things. In this way she will
get everything she wants once she desires this, if her wants are
her husband's wants.

Because so many reject this path, many women today
complain, become agitated, and are unfulfilled. Explanations

are given such as P.M.S., emotional stress, etc. (the point here is not to say P.M.S. or other items are not legitimate medical or physical conditions; that is widely accepted and not rejected in the point being made, rather the point being made is that these conditions are used many times to excuse unchristian behavior), yet saints who were wives and mothers never used these excuses. The women saints were able to handle womanly difficulties because they fulfilled their obligations. Their spirits were at peace, as they patiently fulfilled their vocation of wife and mother to perfection. No women, nor any men for that matter, can be content or at peace with themselves unless they know they are doing their all to fulfill God's call for them. Any less will lead to feelings of inadequacies and blaming of husbands, children, P.M.S., etc. for their troubles that, in many cases, they themselves caused by not carrying out their duties.

Rebellion has a powerful way of showing up a year later in a child when the year before the wife did something against the husband. She then will not understand the chaos in the family and will long for peace. Little situations of self-interest of the wife instead of an urge for the husband come with a big price, and **it is she who suffers the most later** if she does not follow God's ordained order. The price of wrongs always results in life becoming harder, and doing right always results in life becoming "more peaceful."

If the husband disagrees with the wife and understands God is showing his family a certain direction, then for the wife to pout and do things like withhold bedroom privileges, nag, etc. is very sinful and damaging to their marriage. This aspect is so serious that even Scripture addresses it. St. Paul says in 1 Corinthians 7:3–5:

> *"The husband should fulfill his duty toward his wife, and likewise the wife toward her husband. A wife does not have authority over her own body, but rather her husband, and similarly a husband does not have authority over his own body, but rather his wife. Do not deprive each other, except perhaps by mutual consent for a time, to be free for prayer, but then return to one another, so that satan may not tempt you through your lack of self-control."*

While it is wrong for either spouse to deny the other, in most cases it is the wife who withholds herself from her husband. A wife, who denies this right of the husband, does great damage. Rather than helping, she actually encourages and builds resentment in her husband toward her. A wife may think she can deny her husband and gain a victory. While her husband may tire and give in to her wants, he still knows he is to stay with the direction God has shown him. The results of her actions will eventually damage his love and respect for her. On the other hand, if he stands up and does not give in to her threats, she still suffers by her taking this unscriptural action by the great loss of respect and love from her husband. His heart, knowing what is right, cannot hold up long without serious damage. With both accounts, she loses and it is she who will reap a bitter harvest because eventually the relationship will deteriorate and the man, by nature, will be far better off than she. Much greater will be her suffering and rightfully so, since justice has it that the originator of a crime is more guilty. This is not to mention the tragedy which comes to the children because of these actions in tearing down and destroying the harmony in the home. Children **will suffer** where these conjugal relationships are denied because they will perceive the hostility between their parents when this denial is taking place in the bedroom. Because of this hostility, it is highly unlikely the couple will show the minor signs of affection and love in the presence of the children, such as the spouses holding hands, hugging each other, or even standing together or sitting together. The absence of these outward signs will show disorder in the bed and breed insecurity in the children. On the other hand, the manifestation of these minor signs will give children security and the assurance that everything is normal and healthy. It, therefore, is very damaging, not just to the husband and wife relationship, but the children as well and all of society — All this, by what takes place in the secrecy of the bedroom.

A wife should have a completely different reaction than what is stated above when she disagrees with her husband. This will bring about joy. It <u>is</u> that she is to give way lovingly and graciously without a hint of bitterness, only sweetness to his way, and agree with him. We must recall it is God's own words that say in Ephesians 5:22:

> *"Wives should be subordinate to their husbands as to the Lord for the husband is head of the wife just as Christ is head of the Church. As the Church is subordinate to Christ, so wives should be subordinate to their husbands in everything."*

Christ leads the Church. The Church is to agree with Christ. It cannot be said, *"Yes, the Church is to follow Christ, but my husband is not Christ."* It does not matter. It is the "position" as head of the wife that she is to honor, not his personality. God's words are absolute and also must be interpreted in the light of the Scriptures as a whole. It is explicitly clear in God's word, that God Himself expects obedience from the wife to the husband, just as the Church is obedient to Christ. This is emphasized in Scripture not once, but many times. How can there be disagreement in the Church toward Christ? And as the comparison is a mandate from God, how then can the wife usurp the husband and disagree? God not only expects the wife to be in harmony with the husband, but He ex-

pects the wife to <u>agree</u> with the husband. By her doing so, she
will gain great influence with her husband, and the wisdom
she possesses will be drawn upon by him in his decisions. This
will bring about the blending of their wills. Through these actions the husband is far more likely to come to reason if his
decision were wrong. Sweetness produces good fruit.
Threats, especially regarding the bedroom, produce bad fruit.
Pope Pius XI writes:

> *"The house built upon a rock, that is to say on*
> *mutual conjugal, chastity, and strengthened by a*
> *deliberately and constant union of spirit, will not*
> *only never fall away but will never be shaken by*
> *adversity."* [16]

After differences or arguments, conjugal relations are a perfect point for starting over, to forgive and to bring about reconciliation. Sad to say during turmoil, the withholding of
conjugal relations is used to further hostility rather than to
dissipate it by keeping good conjugal relations. Withholding
relations results in a negative outcome, causing more turmoil
and is highly destructive. But what of a bad husband who
does not live right or fulfill his role? As already stated, the
wife is still not excused. She is to be obedient and submissive
in <u>all</u> areas. If she is, even in the midst of adversity, respect
for authority will be continued, which is essential for the
children's security not to be shaken. And if and when the

"center" converts, peace will flow as a river, along its banks, allowing life and villages to flourish; so too will her family by her heroic actions. While she may not be happy in complying with being obedient and submissive in all areas of her life, the wife will fare far better and be happier than if she takes the opposite direction. One has only to look at a recent incident to see how damaging it is to children when parents do not live their roles in harmony. Whether it's from the "bed or the kitchen, *" hostility, coldness and arguments are devastating to children's hearts. Arlene Andrews, a sociology professor at the University of South Carolina, interviewed friends and relatives of Mrs. Susan Smith, who murdered her two children by strapping them in their seatbelts and rolling the car into a lake. The sociologist concluded after the interviews that Mrs. Smith lived two lives — one life as a quiet person with a sweet personality, but another life that was one of "chaos and confusion." Miss Andrews traced some of her problems to arguments and fights between Mrs. Smith's parents while she was growing up as a little girl. These arguments eventually brought on her parents' separation, which resulted in bigger

---

* "Bed or the kitchen" represents everything encompassed in a marriage. In other words, you are going full circle from giving birth, conjugal relationships — the duties of the wife to be fulfilled with joy to another place of importance of a wife and mother, which is the kitchen where she is cooking and cleaning and managing the household. "Bed or the kitchen" encompasses everything in the management and running of a household of family, husband, children, etc.

and more complex problems from which Mrs. Smith was not resilient enough to recover. [17]

Arguments and resentment of any nature are damaging and all incidences which spark them should be eliminated in every way. If it can't be done, then the minimizing of these situations is crucial in order for them not to escalate and transmit severe damage to the children.

"I feel I must contact you and solicit your prayers for a family that is close to me and suffering greatly. Sharon and David were having problems like many families. They were unsure of their roles, having fallen away from the Church with no clear solutions to their problems. When things got really bad, they decided divorce was the answer. They split when their five children were still young. Now, twenty years later, Ted, the oldest of the five, is divorced and has severed all ties with the family. Alex died of AIDS at 26 years old. Robert has been diagnosed with AIDS and is suffering terribly. Karen is divorced and addicted to alcohol and drugs, and Kevin has been missing for eight years.

"Both Sharon and David have remarried and divorced again and today are alone, empty and devastated.

"I know all of this sounds incredible, but this tragic story is real! Please pray for this family!"

*A letter from
Miami, Florida*

CHAPTER SEVEN

WHAT NOT TO DO;
WHAT TO DO

The following are two true examples of how wives who were in bad situations reacted differently, with one producing bad fruit while the other good fruit. It shows God's wisdom in holding us accountable to Scriptures, even if our situations are bad.

"When my parents were divorced, I was about 7 years old and my sisters 5 & 4 years old. The news of the divorce seemed as much of a shock to my mother as it was to all of us. I'll never forget the telephone slipping from her hand, she pacing the floor, praying 'Our Fathers, Hail Mary's' out loud. She experienced a nervous breakdown and was put into a mental institution for about one year. We girls lived with my grandparents. During this time, seeds of hatred toward my father were planted into our hearts. He would show up for a monthly visitation, and my grandmother would go outside and talk to him and come in and tell us he didn't want to

*take us that day. We would feel crushed. He was
our daddy. We missed him. We loved him. When
we did see him, we had fun, but already a wall was
being built between us by what we were <u>taught</u>
about him. We came home from one monthly visitation (a two-hour lunch), bearing gifts. My first
guitar! I was excited! My grandmother quickly gathered us in our bedroom to burst the bubble.
'Your father doesn't love you. He would never
have left you if he did. He never wanted children.
He gave you these things to try to <u>buy</u> your love.'*

"All these years I saw my mother as a complete victim. It wasn't until just before my 29th birthday that
I learned the truth. I visited my dad. With sincerity,
he told me how he would look forward to visitation
time, driving 2 ½ hours to come see us, to be greeted
in the driveway by my grandmother telling him we
weren't home and couldn't see us that month, all the
while we were in the house. When grandma came
in and told us he didn't <u>want</u> to see us, another row
of bricks was laid in the wall of our hearts as we
disappointedly undressed out of our good clothes.*

"Dad told me that early in their marriage, my mother
always desired to be with her mother. When dad saved
enough money, they moved 2 ½ hours away. My moth-*

*er spent long hours on the telephone with her mother
and family during the week. Just about every weekend
she made the trip with us back to visit while dad stayed
home. Dad talked to her about the phone bill, about <u>his
desire to be together</u> as a family; but my mother disobeyed, continuing the phone calls, leaving on weekend
visits. The seeds of disobedience reaped a harvest of sin,
infidelity, hatred. Many lives and hearts shattered.
Years of tears, a childhood robbed of love — all because of one single act of continued disobedience."*

The sin of disobedience of the wife leads to the sin of
the husband. Through her rebellion, she pushed him into the
arms of another woman and he left, losing hope of ever re-
conciling with his wife and eventually with the children. Being blocked from seeing them, he in turn abandoned them.
The weak husband, instead of being strengthened by the love
and obedience of the wife, is weakened further by her opposite actions. The father, wife, and children are all left devastated as the following poem shows. It was written by the
same woman who was the little girl caught in the middle.*

---

* "Caught in the middle" means being caught in the crossfire between two opposing forces
on a battlefield; being caught in the middle of the battlefield.

January 26, 1982

For Dad...... .....who must wonder who I really am.

Dear Daddy

Dear daddy, where are you?
I have grown up so.
Dear daddy, you missed me,
In the school Christmas show.

Dear daddy, you missed when
We had parents' day,
And the time we took care
Of a baby blue-jay.

Dear daddy, where were you
When I fell down and cried?
The love kept for you
Has faded and died.

Dad, how could you go
Without any good-byes?
Everyone tells me
I have your green eyes.

Dear daddy, I'm tired
Of wondering why.
The time that you called,
You made mommy cry.

Dear daddy, you weren't
Around for my prom,
When I left for the shore
Where the waters were calm.

Dear daddy, I've moved out,
I'm living with three;
Eddie and Kate,
And our dog Ebone.

Dear daddy, I hear
You put men behind bars,
You've done that to me
And left deep wounds and scars.

Oh my dear daddy!
Why did you leave?
For the rest of our lives,
Your babies will grieve.

The poem which was written before the meeting with
her father in which she learned what really happened, shows

the devastation of what simple acts of not doing God's will
will lead to. The little girl, now a woman herself, was led into
a life of sin, leaving home at 17, but through Our Lady was
led to reconciliation, not only with her father, but with God
the Father also. Still more, she writes of this whole experience and how now the tables have turned on who was disobedient in the first place, her mother. While even this cannot be justified before God, it is a good warning to mothers
about their awesome responsibilities; what goes around always comes around. She adds:

> *"This experience brings me to the following con-
> clusions:*

> *"Firstly, the power God has bestowed upon
> mothers is truly awesome! How is it, that the
> child of a father who travels, or is a missionary,
> who is not often home, can have a positive opi-
> nion of his daddy? A deep love and affection
> that brings the child wrapped around his daddy's
> knees when he returns from a mission? Who
> keeps that flame of love kindled, but a <u>Mother</u>?*

> *"We mothers as a whole, are so unworthy of the title
> that Our Lady holds in all its fullness and purity of its
> meaning: <u>Mother</u>. The whole heart of the family! A
> mother gives birth, nurtures, mends, heals, brings up,*

loves. God grants these graces to each mother. How have we been stewards of these choice graces?

"The only bitterness I had left in my shadows (which only the light of love has dispelled) is that towards those who wrongly formed my attitude and disposition toward my father. A seed of hatred was planted and nurtured in my heart; now, however, through truth, the same bitterness, hurt, anger, and resentment is toward those who planted the seed. You reap what you sow.

"In retrospect, my mother and grandmother have reaped in a harvest, bountiful in sorrow and misery, in my opinion (formed by the Scriptures) because of their sowing treacherous seeds.

"Sirach 22:22 and 28:3

'A contemptuous insult, a confidence broken, or a treacherous attack will drive away any friend.

'Should a man <u>nourish</u> anger against his fellows and expect healing from the Lord?'"

Love,
New Jersey

The second true example that follows shows a husband who was worse than the husband in the previous example, but through the obedience, holiness, and submission of the wife, a completely different outcome of fruit grew from the marriage. Their now grown son writes:

"I've seen my father drink to excess <u>hundreds</u> of times. I've seen him become abusive, cuss, throw things, fight and even strike my mother. For a time I remember he stopped using her name and would refer to her as 'you' when addressing her. One time I remember wanting so much to ask him why he hated her so much, but fearing for my physical life, I dared not be so bold. Despite all of this, mom would cry from time to time but never would she say an unkind word about him to us, and when we did, she would scold us and say, 'don't be disrespectful, he works very hard to feed us and keep the roof over our heads.'

"Once I remember my father coming home drunk and striking my mother. We were horrified, but my mother turned to us kids and said, 'Don't you <u>dare</u> hold this against your father. It is not him who does this.' My mother's willingness to submit and live for my father held us to-

gether even when we began to grow older and move out.

"In 1977, when I was 17, I remember that my sister was caught in the act of adultery. It had been going on for over a year (her husband's best friend). Her husband gave her a choice — 'him or me.' My sister decided she didn't want to live with her husband anymore. She couldn't stand him. She appeared at my mother's and asked if she and the two children could come move in with her. Mom said, 'Go back to your husband, you belong with him. I can't let you come here.' My sister was shocked and disappointed, then returned home and mom cried bitterly. My sister and her husband reached reconciliation, moved to another state and are together today 18 years later all because of my mother's wisdom.

"On another occasion, my other sister was having a fervent argument with her husband. I overheard her tell my mom that she was withholding 'bedroom privileges' from him until she got her way. My mother immediately told her 'don't you dare do that, you will push him into the arms of another woman and you'll be miserable for the rest of your life.'

*"I'm <u>sure</u> that the way my mother dealt with her
trials, the lesson she taught through her actions,
is the reason why I don't hate my dad today. Not
only that, but it left my heart open to find out
who my dad really was."*

How many wives can learn from this woman's actions
and continue to love and obey their husbands in the midst of
adversity? Who today gives this kind of advice to her children? Our Lady and Her messages reflect exactly this mother's life.

August 30, 1981

Regarding a woman who wants to leave her husband because
he is very cruel to her:

**"Let her remain close to him and accept her
suffering. Jesus, Himself, also suffered."**

As the mother's life in the previous letter produced
fruit and helped make her children whole, so will Our Lady's
messages when followed. What would be the advice today of
friends and family to this mother who was in a bad situation?
*"Divorce him!" "Leave him!" "I wouldn't take that," "With-
hold the bed from him," "Take care of yourself," "Go to a
shelter."* Yet, she did none of these things, and to do anything

other than what she did would have produced the same bad fruit as shown in the first letter. However, the story is not over yet. What follows shows how bad our "judgments" are and the danger of giving advice or interfering <u>with any</u> marriage, other than positive encourage- ment that you must stick it out. In the second letter most are probably against this father and have no sympathy for him because of his treatment of this good wife. However, the son who wrote about his parents did seek out more about his father.

> *(ABOUT THE FATHER) "When he was a little boy of six, he happily ran to his mother with a box containing a whole litter of puppies. With excitement, he exclaimed to her, 'Look!!' Happily he awaited her excitement only to look up from the beautiful little puppies to see the stern look on his mother's face. His joy turned to sorrow, then to grief at what she told him. 'Go drown them in the stream. It is the depression and we can't feed them.' Oh! How his heart sank. How he struggled with her orders. As he turned to carry them down the trail, she said, 'and hold them under the water until no more bubbles come out.' He thought, why did he, a little boy, have to do such a thing? It wasn't like killing a chicken for food. These were his friends. He arrived beside the water, grabbed the*

*first one with both hands, kissed him, and said he
was sorry. As he leaned over the water, he could
see the reflection of himself holding the puppy.
Rippling the water as he placed it under the water, it felt horrible as it wiggled in his soft hands
that were supposed to be feeding and petting it.
Hands that were supposed to be licked were now
used instead to drown it. The pain he felt as he
held it under the water was more than a tender
six year old heart could stand. When at last he
could no longer feel or see it wiggling, he lifted it
out of the water. His eyes, as wet as the drowned
puppy, could hardly see the little limp body
which, just before, was so wildly jumping and
playing. He laid it on the bank and seeing the
contrast of death and life of the other puppies
playing made it just as difficult the second time.
He did the whole scene a third, fourth, fifth time,
until the whole litter lay there before him. It
would lie in his memory every night for a long
time and even become more horrible for him in
the future.*

*"Four years had passed and now he had a little
sister. He was her big brother, her protector, a
big ten-year-old to his little sister of only three.
They were playing outside. Back then there were*

*no septic tanks, rather cesspools, and he and his
sister had been playing around them. Later
when they came home, they became sick. When
they were taken to the doctor's, he told them that
they had an infection (virus) and the best way to
help them was to drink no water. So the parents
turned the water off to the house to be sure and
follow the doctor's orders. After the first day,
they both were very thirsty. The boy's burning
thirst the next day was unquenchable. He knew
how to turn the water on but resisted until he
could no longer do so. He turned it on just long
enough to take a drink. He didn't want to get his
sister in trouble so he wouldn't give her any
though he wanted to. Later that day, she went
alone to the bathtub. She tried and tried to suck
the water from the faucet, knowing water came
out there. She turned on the faucet only to find it
dry. She was on fire for water, so thirsty she felt
she could die. Sometime later, her big brother,
her buddy, came in. What he saw killed his little
heart. Four years before he killed the litter of
puppies by too much water and before him now,
he killed his sister by giving her no water. She
lay dead in the tub in her last effort to suck water
from the dry faucet. The doctor had actually*

misdiagnosed the remedy and what was really
needed was plenty of water.

"It didn't matter if he had been told by someone
else to drown the puppies. It didn't matter that
he had been told not to drink water or give his
sister any. He, for the rest of his life, would hear
the accusing voice inside his head — If only
when I got a drink....If only....

"Later still, World War II came along. He, a
young man now, entered the war. He endured
one of the bloodiest battles, Iwo Jima, in the
South Pacific, where blood flowed like 'water.'
Married by now, the wife who was to stick beside
him, her husband, for better or for worse, said
upon his return from Iwo Jima, 'Something died
inside of him on that island.' He never talked
about what he experienced and it remains a mys-
tery to the wife and children. But they all now
know it was the final death of his spirit to live
normally. These three instances would affect
him for the rest of his life. So many times he
*would 'drown' himself with **liquor** as he did the*
*puppies in the **water**, the absence of **water** with*
*his sister, and the blood, flowing as **water**, in Iwo*
Jima; to him all he could see, in all three situa-

*tions, was his reflection as in the **water** of the*
stream long ago."

The son who tells all this writes:

> *"Looking back, he tried to keep his kids pure, he*
> *detested pornography, he hated television, he*
> *never missed Sunday Mass, and I saw him pray*
> *many times when he thought he was alone. The*
> *litter of puppies and his sister's death devastated*
> *him. I know this hurt him so badly because he*
> *would bring it up so many times when he was*
> *drinking.*

> *"My father was killed in a crane accident in 1975*
> *and yet for all his faults, I know he is in Heaven.*
> *My mother saved my brothers, sisters, and my*
> *heart, and I firmly believe my father's salvation*
> *is due to her being a perfect wife and mother."*

How many men not only leave the home but are eternally lost because their wives, by their selfishness, nagging, or disposition, brought them down instead of bringing them up by their submission, affection, respect. Many today may say, *"What about men? Why place it upon the women?"* It is ordained by God that all boys and girls come through the woman. It is she who is charged with forming their little hearts

under the guidance of the husband, by having far more time
to spend with them. It is she who teaches them, first, how to
love and cuddle when in the middle of the night, tired, she
rises and holds her child to her breast not just to feed him but
in those first months of life to let him "feel" mother; her
closeness, her soothing hums and lullabies.

It is she who forms the image of his father in her little
one, saying, *"Your father is doing his best." "I am able to get
up in the middle of the night and feed you because he works
and keeps a roof over our head." "I am proud to be his wife."*
No greater security will the child have than to know this, even
when the child becomes aware of faults in his father. The so-
lidness of respect and admiration will still hold for the father
and the more faults a father has, the more respect and admiration will come back to the mother by the child, because the
child will come to the age of reasoning and will be grateful to
the mother for loving his father in the midst of his faults. The
child may, too, actually love and respect her more, knowing
she chose to love as the beautiful example given in the second
letter shows. It is women who are to break the cycle of bad
mothers and fathers which now plague our society, as Our
Lady's message showed when She blessed specifically only
the mothers.

It is the men, once women will allow themselves to
submit to them, who will guide the direction. Without their

submission, society will continue its spiritual and physical downfall. The woman, in her wisdom and through her prayers, will pull out the best in man. A woman will never better her condition by nagging, compromising her husband's judgements, ridiculing, etc.; rather she will create a war or a situation of driving the husband into hobbies and away from the home, or just to walk away completely. Scripture states:

Galatians 5:15

"If you go on biting and tearing one another to pieces, take care! You will end up in mutual destruction."

"I have just made my first marriage retreat and something really hit my heart hard as I heard these words spoken. The speaker said, 'Husbands <u>look</u> at your wives, wives <u>look</u> at your husbands — one day, maybe not to far from now, one of you will be looking at the other in a coffin.' Wow, I thought, what would she say — would she grieve or would she be relieved?"

CHAPTER EIGHT

WOE TO AN ABUSIVE HUSBAND

The wife and mother is to make the home a "haven" for the husband, a place that rather than dreading going home to, he will long for. His home should be his heaven. Yes, many times, the wife will suffer, especially if the husband is not submitting to God's divine promptings, but she, doing her best, will not be without God's favors being showered upon her, many times in her sufferings, purchasing the grace for her husband to convert, change and become a better father. <u>Woe</u> to the husband whose wife is guiltless and petitions the Lord. **While it is he, the husband, who exercises his authority over the wife, it is God the Father who deals His authority over the husband.** It is God the Father Who will answer the petition of a wife whose tears He will dry, by dealing directly with the husband, or by the husband's losing the blessing of protection of God the Father, thereby, permitting satan to harm him, as the following letter shows. While reading, remember this letter was written by a daughter who greatly admires her mother.

Dear Caritas of Birmingham,   *Feb. 8, 1994*

"I would like to share with you a painful story, but maybe you can use it somewhere, somehow. While I was growing up, I saw my father change from a very devoted family man, loving father, to an abusive, violent alcoholic. My mother tells us this change lasted seven years. During these seven years, my mother prayed to God to cure him or come and get him. My mother never entertained the thought of leaving because she lived the way our Blessed Mother asked and still asks all of us to live. She remained faithful to her husband even when she kept getting pregnant; she never refused him. We were a large family of 14 children. I was the fourth oldest and remember much of the good times and all of the bad times. Even today, my mother never speaks ill of my father, who, before he died had smashed my mother's head in with a hammer, nearly killing her. He died while running away from the scene. The police said he passed out at the wheel and hit a rock cut.

"I don't think women should have to suffer this much in our society, but my mother was the best model of living her vows 'for better or worse.'

She really truly 'loved.' She never bad mouthed
my dad, but made us understand that it was al-
cohol which made him this way. My mother is
okay today. She lives a simple life. She is 65
years young and this incident happened when she
was 36 years old with 14 children to care for.

"Today, I thank God for all the people who are
doing the right thing to bring people back to
God. Some are harder to move than others.
Their hearts are so hard because of the hurt they
have suffered. I must trust in Our Blessed Moth-
er's intervention and God's mercy. I pray for you
all, and I ask that you pray for all my family."

Meaford, Ontario, Canada

While this may anger some, it must be recalled that it is
the daughter who states: *"but made us understand,"* and it is
the daughter writing who still can refer to him as *"My father"*
as she writes. This indicates the mother, by her actions, protected the children from corrosive hatred.

While it would seem justified in saying *"leave this*
man," the fact that she didn't gave such a testimony to the
children that this woman is able to live a healed life with her
children. <u>While this kind of violence cannot be condoned in</u>

any way, the fact that she loved and obeyed opened the door
for all of her children not to be permanently damaged, though
scarred. The husband's sins were offset by the mother's love.
This prevented the children from hating, which is far more
damaging than the damage they received by being witnesses
to the abuse. Her example to her children, actually in the
end, will have a "certain" positive effect on the children's future, teaching them to live out their commitments under the
most adverse conditions. These are the elements which
formed the early Christian martyrs. Love your enemy and
make a commitment to Christ. She continued to love her
husband, who made himself an enemy, and committed herself
to the vow she made before Christ. Yes, it was through the
martyrdom of this mother and even the blood she shed, that
brought the possibility of a certain amount of healing to her
family which had been severely damaged by this tragedy.
However, it would have been completely destroyed by divorce. Divorce brings about hatred and bitterness. Hatred
destroys everything. The wife, as well as the children, would
have been injured in their hearts far more by hatred than by
the abuse. Are we stating here that it is okay for women to be
abused? Of course not! That would be a ridiculous conclusion from these writings. Rather what is being stated is we
must look to God for a solution about how to pull good from
tragedy. We must follow Our Lady's messages when She says

to abandon <u>everything</u> to God when we are in difficult situations.

January 2, 1989

> "...In this new year I want to give you peace; I want to give you love and harmony. Abandon all your problems and all your difficulties to me. Live my messages. Pray, pray!"

and...

March 28, 1985

> "Dear children, today I wish to call you to pray, pray, pray! In prayer you shall perceive the greatest joy and the way out of every situation that has no exit..."

and...

July 25, 1989

> "Dear children, today I am calling you to renew your heart. Open yourself to God and surrender to Him all your difficulties and crosses so God may turn everything into joy..."

and...

June 29, 1992

**"Dear children, tonight in a special way I want
to invite you to surrender completely to me.
Give me all your problems and difficulties..."**

This woman's vows were so sacred to her that she
risked everything not to break the vow she made before God,
just as St. Agnes chose death rather than losing her virginity.
This woman's heroic act of standing in the face of death rather than breaking and losing her vow is in union with the
saints. So many today lack an understanding of the spirit of
the saints, and when the least abuse comes up, it is used to jus-
tify leaving. This woman's life stands as an **<u>indictment</u>** and
<u>witness</u> for all other women who are ready to call it quits for
far less abuse such as "mental abuse" or even non-life threat-
ening physical abuse, etc. We know this will anger some
women just to see what was just stated, but it is time we re-
learn the spirit of trial and perseverance. It is precisely this
reason why Our Lady told the woman who suffered cruelty at
the hands of the husband to:

August 30, 1981

"Let her remain close to him and accept her suffering. Jesus, Himself, also suffered."

This message cannot simply be passed off as, *"Oh, but this is just an isolated case,"* because every message of Our Lady's is of grave importance; statements of truth, of a correct way to live, and of Heaven's desires. The messages do not apply singularly, even when given singularly as was the case with this message. There is a teaching here for all marriages, of what is Heaven's view and Our Lady's spiritual counseling for those who find themselves in bad situations to further grasp the weight of the above message. It also is important to understand that the definition of "<u>cruel</u>" in former Yugoslavia is many degrees worse than how we would define it. Their normal life was lived under the harshness and cruelty of Communism. The way they treated their animals, many in this country would define as cruelty, but all this is the normal level of life for them. The recent civil war showed the cruelty these people can be capable of if they are abusive. So the point being made is if anyone requested a visionary to ask Our Lady to leave because of cruelty of the husband, you can rest assured she was suffering real cruelty, real abuse. Our Lady clearly confirms through Her answer that she grasped that the woman was not suffering in a minor way but perhaps severely, for Our Lady places her in union with Jesus saying

"Jesus, Himself, also suffered."   Again, it is necessary here to be repetitive because some will misquote and take out of context from these writings the point being made. <u>Abuse is wrong!</u> We are not dealing with the fact that it should never take place, that is clear. Rather we are dealing with once it does, what our reaction should be, and Our Lady tells us clearly. Are we saying, then, a woman should let an abusive husband kill her? <u>No!</u> We are saying when you suffer pray, live purely, and put it in God's hands. <u>God will remedy. He will rescue</u>, as was the case of the woman in the previous letter. Scripture states:

Psalms 91:12

> *"For God commands the angels to guard you*
> *in all your ways. With their hands, they shall*
> *support you..."*

We have forgotten this. We have come up with our solutions to these tragedies. Women's shelters are a sign of disease, of not just abuse but the fact that we no longer rely on God as the foregoing Scripture promises. We seek human solutions. Seeking human solutions in almost all cases in today's society encourages separation, which leads to disunity, and results in a totally dysfunctional family as opposed to a partially dysfunctional family. A partially dysfunctional family leaves the possibility of healing, while a totally dysfunctional family (divorced) removes any chance of recovery. The need of being family is so powerful in the human heart that even children, when removed from abuse they themselves suffer, will later choose to go right back into that same family situation. The probation officer quoted earlier said:

> *"We have removed children from parents who have abused them and placed these children in foster families who offer love and a normal life, even swimming pools, etc., only to see them six months later choose to go back into their situations."* [18]

Again the point here is not to excuse the abuse of children or that we should ignore it, rather to show how the human heart longs for family more than any other craving. Because of that, a mother and father must do <u>everything</u> necessary to keep the family intact even if situations are not perfect, at the same time without compromising their roles, even if it is only one spouse who lives his or her role. This one spouse will teach the children perseverance and commitment.

The mother of the fourteen children lived her vows as her daughter said for "better or worse." She also lived Our Lady's messages perfectly, even before she knew of Our Lady's messages. Rather than take the matter into her own hands, she did as the saints did, surrendering everything to

God <u>because</u> she depended on God. He brought about a remedy. By the father's refusing God's grace, satan took action
and led him to death. This warning should strike fathers. For
those mothers who are praying and are pure "are" reaching
Heaven. Living purely and righteously, these heroines are a
perfect witness for those mothers who think their rebellion is
excused by the husband's behavior. Many men's salvation is
in the hands of a loving wife. It is quite possible that the father killed in the car crash may have gained at least purgatory
because of the wife's sufferings. While obviously satan struck,
no judgement can be made with regard to his salvation. How
many friends, family members, and now, sad to say, even
priests have told mothers to leave, which may have in turn
doomed husbands when followed through.

These writings were published first in the Caritas of
Birmingham newsletter, November 1994 – December 1995.
Thousands of letters came in responding to these writings.
Letters ran 50 – 1 in favor of what you are now reading.
Many people wrote stating that after putting into practice
what was published, their lives changed. Husbands began to
change, to treat their wives and families better. Since this
book was in the process of being printed, we added the following letter, which does not appear in the original printing.
It is a representation of many other letters we received and
confirms all that you just read.

Good Morning!   *February, 1996*

"I have just finished reading your book — there is so much to absorb. Most of it has really touched me deeply — perfect timing to start Lent and God has given me so much to work on and pray about through this.

"My husband went through a terrible time over ten years ago, and I prayed so hard for my children's safety and my own. My husband often threatened and used verbal abuse, and I just prayed for the precious Blood protection over our family. Many asked me to leave him. But when I prayed, God led me to Scripture that said 'stay,' and an evangelist I heard said, 'God has a message for someone in a troubled marriage. He will watch over you and protect you and you are not to leave your husband. A Christian woman will lead her husband back to the Lord — by trusting God and believing in Him.' I prayed for God to change my husband and one day, months later, my answer finally came. God spoke inside and said — 'I can't change him, but you can change.' I cried out first — 'What more can you ask of me?' I was to look at my husband through the eyes of a loving God and love him

and accept him just as he was. God forgave me my sins and accepted and loved me before I changed — so I needed to do this for my husband.

"It was hard at first, but I started cooking especially to please him and treated him with respect. For nine months we had been like cold bricks. I did not respect him, and now I see where I tore my family apart. But after about two months, <u>God healed</u> our family. I did not understand much of what happened until reading this book. God worked us through this very thing ten years ago and has blessed us.

"My husband has so much wisdom. I spoke to him very briefly about this book, and he told me so much that you have written and I had never understood. God has blessed me with a wonderful husband, whom I am only beginning to understand. I am so glad I did not listen to others and walk away from him.

"I thank you for writing this book. My two daughters do not obey and respect their husband and fiancé. I have tried to explain this need to do so and prayed for them now that you have writ-

*ten it so well. Thank you for all your prayers
and hard work."*

Perham, Minnesota

We, as a society, must fight separation — not just divorce.
We must bring out the truths about family, of how God wants
the family to run, by submitting to His order through the father to the mother and then the mother to the children. This
parallels God's order down to the smallest particle of the
atom.

Dear Friend of Medjugorje,

"I have been reading your book on <u>How to Change Your Husband</u>*, and wish this had been available for me ten years ago when I was having very difficult times with my first husband, the father of our two children. I sought counseling from professionals and our parish priest who knew us both. After hearing my story, he, too, felt that I was in an unholy marriage but could not advise me of a divorce which I was not asking him to do. To make a long story short, however, later I was granted a divorce and an annulment from the Church after almost twenty years of marriage.*

"Amazingly, all seemed well with all of us for two years — until I remarried a good, moral and Catholic man (My first husband was very anti-religion). Within a year my 20-year-old son returned with his father, filled with much hate and contempt for me; and my daughter returned this past year to live with her dad for her last two years of high school. The emotional pain has been incredible for me to bear since I know that I did not abandon my children but rather their father lured them with promises and lies which I refused to do. I must admit that I am trying to forgive my ex-husband but it is so hard to do. I really need help with this…unfortunately, your book has caused me more pain since I now feel that I should have stayed with him at all costs since I was the only one suffering in that marriage. I really thought that it was 'best for the children' and was told by professionals the same.

"Now I know the past cannot be changed. I must live in the present. What does Our Lady say to people like me — people who did not stay with the original partner and are now remarried in the Church to a wonderful man? What is to become of us who unwittingly made bad decisions and cannot go back and change them? I need help going forward with my life and the lives of my children and husband. How does one bring broken families together again?"

Knoxville, Tennessee

CHAPTER NINE

GOD HATES DIVORCE
(Malachi 2:16)

One individual, who heard of a Christian couple's plans for divorce, was so fed up and disgusted about hearing of Christian divorces that he wrote the following to them even though he did not know them:

Dear Friend,

"I was told of your plans for divorce and wrote the following for you. It doesn't matter whether I know the circumstances or not. Divorce does not work.

The Problem and the Solution

"Divorce is chosen as a solution to a problem — the 'answer' when things can't be worked out. Once chosen and what seemed to be the way out is really a deception. Rather than an answer, it will bring about a host of more and bigger problems in your life, complicating and entangling you. Kids do not sur-

vive this as a flu in which for a short time they will be sick and recover. No, they will be severely crippled and damaged for the rest of their lives. Robbed of the one thing they hold in life more than any other, that is the security of being raised in a home of two individuals who through the miracle of conception, made them 'one being' from two, having both the father and mother in their very self. To tear the marriage vow apart through divorce is to tear the heart out of the child. Terrible violent destruction follows for all involved. Nurtured along by the hands of satan whom then you will recognize for what he did, but who was there in the beginning, disguised as your conscience, a friend, or family member, whispering softly, gently, ever so sweetly:

…"'Divorce….Divorce….It is the solution….It will bring peace….peace….find peace….divorce….'

"It is a tragedy that no one listens to Jesus instead; that prayer is the solution."

         Praying for you,

         A friend violently opposed in spirit to your plans and scandal.

It is **today** that Our Lady wants us to change radically; for fathers to begin submitting to the will and precepts of God; for wives to do so with their husbands, in everything; for us to challenge every form of separation; to speak boldly against those who advise or lead to "the coming apart" or "expecting the family to operate with no center." The family is not a democracy. While the husband is not to be a dictator, he is still the ruler, the king, and the wife, the queen.

Even minds who are not Christian recognize, by their spirit, the truth and importance of family structure and the peace which ensues. One of the greatest minds of all time writes:

> "The rule of the household is a monarchy, for every house is under one head."

> Aristotle 384–322 BC

However, today the danger lies not so much in the husband being a dictator, but rather in the wife being one. Aristotle compared the husband-wife relationship to the one-sided relationship between soul and body in which the soul, the husband, must rule, not be ruled. How is it that this ancient mind believed these truths? Is not a soul, since it is from God, capable of hearing its Maker's divine prompting? Can a father also guide his family by submitting his life to the Father? Yet women today are rebellious to this. One husband wrote:

> *"My wife wanted to take a direction that clearly I*
> *understood from God was not what He wanted*
> *for my family. She insisted to the point of saying*
> *she would leave. I, in turn told her to go ahead.*
> *I would not go contrary to what God has made*
> *me understand."*

Is it going to take this kind of strong reaction from fathers for society's direction to be straightened out? While more and more fathers are beginning to take charge, there are also more and more women who are having the desire to live what Scripture says. The following is a letter we received from a woman who related **her** desires to live Scripture and her own journey from rebellion to an understanding of the good fruit that comes to a family when submission is accepted and practiced by the wife in a marriage:

> *Dear Caritas,*   *June, 1995*
>
> *"I began to change my 'worldly' view about*
> *submission when my husband was on his first*
> *trip to Medjugorje. We were praying a special*
> *novena to St. Theresa about discernment over a*
> *move that would seriously change the direction*

of our whole family financially, physically and spiritually. During this novena, I began to open up Scripture, and every time, I kept reading verses about a wife's role; particularly I recall the one about 'wives be submissive to your husbands.' That was always a 'turn-off' verse to me! I always considered 'submissive' a demeaning, 'lower' word. Little did I know what a 'HIGH-ER' calling it really is.

*"Through this novena, it dawned on me that I did not really need to pray for discernment, but that I would yield to my husband's discernment — **YES**, I would be **submissive** to his discernment! After changing my prayer request that God lead my husband in **his** discernment, with my compliance, I discovered a release, a sense of new found freedom — just the <u>**opposite**</u> of what my idea of submission was all about! Really, this was very enlightening to me.*

"In smaller steps I began yielding to his decisions and found that it always did seem to work out better that way — a more peaceful way with a sense of harmony. It's not like I didn't have any input; on the contrary, I found that my input became more valuable to him in his decision-making. <u>Now</u> it is

*'input' and 'suggestions,' and not 'nagging!' It's
hard to explain but the relationship and the family
just flows when the 'order' is right.*

*"This also lead me to discover and realize more of
my own role of how a mother sets the 'mood' and
'atmosphere' for the entire family. I discovered this
the hard way (the way I'm most familiar with!)
My husband would come home from work after a
stressful day, with good intentions of unwinding a
bit and playing with the kids while I made dinner,
but a lot of factors would block his good intentions. He would come in, and one or two (or
more!) of the kids would be crying because they
were hungry 'NOW' or wanted to report to daddy
all the 'misdeeds' of the day. Often the kids would
be blasting their children's tapes (which get on his
nerves even when they're low) and he'd probably
trip over toys and clutter on the living room floor
in his efforts to get to one of the children. It often
wound up in him losing his patience completely,
and created a tense dinner atmosphere.*

*"After this routine happened enough times, I
asked myself, 'How can I change this?' I realized that I could find out what time he was going
to come home. About one hour before that, I*

*give the kids a small snack so they won't be cry-
ing when he comes in. After that, they must pick-
up the living room floor. I try to get them doing
something they'll be peaceful at, awaiting the
moment daddy comes home. Close to the time of
his arrival I let them know that daddy's going to
be home any time in order to try to make that
moment a real awaited for and excited time.
Sometimes I play soft music, but I've found it's
usually better quiet. I even try to make sure dinner smells good for when he walks in.*

*"When my husband comes in the door, on these
planned-ahead days, the kids will all say 'DAD-
DY!!!' all at the same time — it's a boost for him.
I've noticed that on these days, they are more apt to
want to tell him the positive events of the day rather
than the negative! Some days are smoother than
others and it's not always 'The Walton's' but it has
made a definite marked improvement. My husband has noticed and appreciates the difference.
Women should realize that it's not just a physical
atmosphere they are gifted to set (clean house, get
togethers, tables) but emotional as well."*

*God Bless!
Hannibal, Missouri*

The above letter is not an isolated case. More and more mothers are writing of insights they are receiving about their roles of wives and mothers since Medjugorje entered their lives, as the following again gives witness to:

Dear Caritas,   *July 15, 1995*

"After speaking to some of your community members and reading your material it has lead me to think of my past as a child and how I live out my faith as an adult today. I can say I am very secure and have a real sense of self-confidence because of being brought up in a real house of love. My parents were always together on their direction for myself, my brother and other sisters. We could never play one against the other because they stood on solid ground together. I can remember only one time knowing my parents were in disagreement with each other. They always kept their problems behind closed doors as far as I could see. My parents had a great love and respect for each other and still have that today. Knowing that they loved each other fostered in me a realization of having no doubt of their love for me.

"It's hard to see in the midst of your life as a teenager how this environment would carry over to

my married life but it certainly has. I remember my mom always, always greeting my dad with a kiss on his return home from work — which in turn we kids took turns kissing him too.

"I am now married and have five kids of my own and know that this love I was shown has in turn shown me how to love my husband and children. I am not perfect in my care for him nor claim one very close to this but my day is certainly highlighted when my husband walks through the front door. I anticipate him coming home. I prepare dinner with love and at least get the house in order and let the kids know their dad is to return home soon. I don't burden him with my affairs of the day but lend an ear to alleviate his worries and frustrations of the day. I want him to find a real place of peace, home in my arms of love and compassion. I greet him with joy and make it easy for him to come home. I try to have my hair combed and lipstick on then, even if I haven't had the chance to comb my hair all day.

"These things may be nothing but I want simply to show him how much I love and value him in my life. I will continue to pray for all of you. Thank

you for your encouraging words written in your newsletters. They are certainly life changing."

Sincerely, a Friend
Pensacola, Florida

Even with these desires of women wanting to live the biblical truths concerning their wifehood and motherhood, it is not an easy road to take. The two women who wrote the above letters must protect themselves in their desire to submit. And from whom should they protect themselves? Strange though it may be, **from other women!**

"I just wanted to say I'm very sorry for all my past sins (many, many) — some serious. I feel the book <u>How to Change Your Husband</u> is right, but it was and is very difficult for me to change my pattern of thinking. I guess Eve's sin really left her mark on me."

A letter from
Palatine, Illinois

CHAPTER TEN

ONE BAD APPLE BROUGHT DOWN ALL OF MAN! IT'S TRUE — ONE BAD APPLE INFECTS THE WHOLE BUNCH!

Many, who want to live what Scripture says about submission, are weakened in their desires and actions by so many rebellious women and society at large who **"infect"** those who wish to submit to their husbands.

In the Bible in the book of "Esther," King Ahasuerus ruled over 120 provinces from India to Ethiopia. While theologians do not say this is a historic account, it pronounces the truths of God. In 482 B.C., the third year of his reign, the king summoned all officials, nobles, and governors from every province. For 180 days the king showed to all the "glorious" riches of his kingdom and the splendid wealth of his royal estate. He governed the whole known world. At the end of the 180 days, there was a feast for 7 days. Gold and silver couches were on the pavement which was of marble and colored stones. Royal wine flowed freely and the feast reflected the king's magnificence. Meanwhile, his Queen Vashti gave a feast for the women inside the royal palace. On the 7th day, the king summoned his queen to his presence, wearing the royal crown so all the officials and populace from all the provinces who had gathered there from all over the known world could behold her beauty. Queen Vashti refused his royal order and would not come. King Ahasuerus was furious but was just and always sought counsel. He ran his kingdom with a form of government and laws. The king conferred with his wise men who were versed in the law because the King's business was conducted in general consultation with lawyers and jurists. He then summoned seven ranking officials and asked, *"What is to be done by law with Queen Vashti for disobeying my orders?"* A ranking official answered, *"The queen has not wronged the king alone, but all the officials and the populace of the king. The queen's conduct will become known to all women and they will look with disdain upon their husbands when it is reported that the queen is disobedient. This very day, ladies who hear of the queen's conduct will rebel against all royal officials with disdain and rancor as the queen. If it pleases the king, issue a decree forbidding Vashti to come into the presence of the King and we authorize the king to give her royal dignity to one more worthy than she."* The decree went out so that by this example, Queen Vashti's disobedience would not **"infect"** the whole kingdom and that all wives would in turn honor their husbands from the greatest to the least. The decree went out that every man should be lord in his own home. Hence the kingdom was saved.

Later, the king's servant suggested that a virgin be sought for a new queen. Various steps of elimination took place from a large number of virgins, leaving seven remaining virgins from which the king would choose one. The king, with wisdom, spent 12 months and several interviews to pick the one who was to be granted queenship over the whole empire. Esther, who was very beautiful and an Israelite in secret, asked for virtually nothing when before the king. She won his favor through submission, tenderness, and no desire for herself. She gained everything and great influence with the king. She was chosen as the new queen and they married. She was repeatedly asked by her husband what she wanted and it would be granted. In her submission she only returned his question with the request that a banquet be held for him. He delighted in her and wanted to give more to her. It was through her wisdom to live as a noble wife, making her husband's wants her own that she gained more influence with her husband, resigned to be under her husband's authority rather than equal to him or over him. Meanwhile, Haman, the king's highest ranking official, plotted to kill all the Jews in all 120 provinces on a single day. Haman desired to do this because Modecai, a Jew also in the king's court, would not bow down to him. The new Queen Esther was Modicai's adopted daughter. She learned of the plot. The queen then gave the king another banquet at which, in his delight with her good-ness, he offered her any request, even half the kingdom. She asked that the decree issued against all Jews on a single day be reversed and the plotters be dealt with by their own origi-nal orders against the Jews. Hence, Haman was executed and throughout all 120 provinces Jews rose up in respect and power, while many others converted to Judaism.

Through the disobedience of Queen Vashti, a whole kingdom was almost lost through her **infectious** rebellion. Through Queen Esther's submission and obedience, a whole nation of people throughout the known world was lifted up.

The young girls on retreat, as mentioned in Chapter Three, reflect a perversion within most of society, an infection of "no man will lord over me." How sad it is that this will be exactly the case as with Queen Vashti, who lost everything through her rebellious disobedience, while Queen Esther rose above her by subjecting herself to her husband. This infec-tious nature starts with Eve and the apple. Symbolic though it may be, this apple she ate of was rotten with evil, infecting her through her actions and desires. It is a fact today that 30 ap-ples in a basket which are fresh, beautiful and ripe will remain so for a reasonable amount of time. Yet, to place one rotten apple in the basket will rapidly spread rottenness throughout the whole bunch. The apple in the Garden of Eden is a per-fect symbol of its infection spreading throughout the whole human race. The king's court knew the rebellion of Queen Vashti would infect all the women of the kingdom. It is of great value to meditate on the simple proverb of *"one bad apple spoils the whole bunch."* Today's society is infected with rebellion and it spreads as a rotten evil.

A woman who was to marry a man with questionable virtues was trying to convince the minister she would bring him up and make him better. The minister told her to stand up on the coffee table. He then said, *"Now lift me up on the table with you."* She struggled, pulled, tried but could not lift him up. After a few moments he simply jerked her with ease off the table, pulling her down to where he stood. He told her, *"It's much easier to be pulled down than to lift someone up."* Women must guard themselves. **Sever relationships** with other wives who are rebellious. Distance yourselves from all who are not willing to summit to God's authority. If wives do not do this they will be infected with the same rebellion which is so rampant in society.

A CHILD'S CRY

Where've you been?
Are you hidin'? Where
can they be? Why am I
cryin'? Is the future more
than me? Nobody's home.

Come home from
school. It's cold and rainy.
Wish there were cookies
momma's bakin'. This day-
care center's not for me.
Nobody's home.

A child cries for
parents. The time's a
changin'. Is the future
worth it all? It's makin'
lots of money for daddy's
car, mom's home. No
one's ever here, and I'm
alone.

Look out the win-
dow, see mom comin'. I
wash my tears; she'll wonder why I'm cryin'. Make
like I've had lots of fun.
Daddy didn't get scared.
I'm scared.

A child cries for
parents. The times a changin'. Is the future worth it
all? It's makin' lots of
money for daddy's car,
mom's home. No one's ev-
er here, and I'm alone.

Where've you been?
Are you hidin'? Where
can they be? Why am I
cryin'? Is the future more
than me? Nobody's home.

No one's ever
home......

Sung by Dennis Agrigino

106

CHAPTER ELEVEN

A CHILD'S CRY

Infectious rebellion is promoted and packaged in many ways. For example, all society is teaching men and women to go to college, get a career, and yes, get married and then both can work. All the while society is deteriorating from the lack of mothers being at home. We say, *"We need the money." "My wife makes more than I do,"* or, *"I make more than my husband." "We can't afford our house payment without both of us working."* All of these are excuses which can be easily remedied. A known football player, who came from nothing into big money, immediately built an expensive home with a $12,000 monthly mortgage. He also purchased cars, vacation homes, etc., only to find by the year's end he was hardly able to pay his bills. Everything is relative. If you make a lot of money, you spend a lot of money. If you make little, you spend little. If a wife and husband have to move out of their four-bedroom home to buy an acre in the country and into a two-bedroom home so she can quit working, then that is what has to happen. In fact, it would be far, far better for a mother to be at home, living in a mobile home on a few acres than to have a nice house, nice car, and the children in day care. The former would produce riches and peace in the family; the latter is a <u>guaranteed</u> future problem and disaster. One family did just that, moving into a mobile home with their three children and had enough extra income by greatly reducing their standard of living that over the next eight years they were able to build a beautiful home and pay cash as they built. The wife gardened and was a homemaker the whole time. We, as Christians, must frown on careers for mothers. How can it be viewed favorably by God when a mother, within a month or two of having a child, places him in someone else's care? God made it so that even a cow doesn't leave its calf until much later than that. Woe to the father who requires his wife to work outside the home. **Children being placed in day care is a prostitution of motherhood.** While many have unconsciously fallen into this trap, it is Our Lady who now comes to enlighten our faults. Yes, we have made big mistakes. All of us have. No one is to be condemned for them, but we must realize Our Lady is repeatedly starting off Her messages with the word **"Today."** Our Lady makes a special statement in this, that, yes, you have tangled yourself up. You are trapped, enslaved, but as of **"Today"** begin to live my messages, and I, with time, will slowly free you. Our Lady knows you have made bad choices, and they are easily forgiven and in time will be rectified, but from this point forward, we are responsible in that we must change our situation. **It is understandable that once these truths are known, you will**

**suffer because many situations which exist cannot be imme-
diately remedied. Our Lady understands this, but expects us
to take steps to change <u>today</u>.** While a mother, after reading
this, may want to quit her job immediately, she may not be
able to. The entanglement of the world will not suddenly free
you when you want it. But with time, prayer, and fasting, Our
Lady will guide you and your husband. Your goal should be
to make a home.

A home is sacred, a noble place where order is born.

*"There is nothing nobler or more admirable than
when two people who see eye to eye keep house
as man and wife, confounding their enemies and
delighting their friends."*

Homer 800–700 B.C.

The only way to have a noble home and see eye to eye
is to understand your roles and live them. The blending of
wills can occur when one understands the concept of God's
ordered structure. By this means, society will change. What
takes place in the home has an important effect upon the
whole world. If homes become unstable, the whole of society
will also. Just as if little atoms throughout the universe were
to break down, this would likewise cause disorder in the universe. It is for this reason the home is sacred, a holy place, a

refuge where the Holy Spirit wishes to dwell in the midst of family.

July 3, 1989

> **"Dear children, your Mother asks you tonight, you, who are present** (people were present from all over the world)**, when you get back into your home, renew prayer in your family. Take time for prayer, dear children. I, as your Mother, especially want to tell you that the family** has to pray **together. The Holy Spirit wants to be present in the families. Allow the Holy Spirit to come. The Holy Spirit comes through prayer. That is why, pray and allow the Holy Spirit to renew you, to renew today's family. Your Mother will help you."**

A house is an empty place built for people to stay in. A home is spiritual, a place in which you live that is sacred, a place that must be created. A well ordered home is necessary to make the angels free to come and go in a place they could recognize as Heaven. The home should be made the place the husband longs to come home to, a place of peace. If the wife doesn't create this peace, but instead creates a place of turmoil, the husband will come home only through duty rather than through love. The natural result of this is the waning of his affection toward his wife.   In the book **Pathway of Life,** it states:

> *"...no woman can long preserve affection if she is negligent in this point — be still more attentive in ornamenting your mind with meekness and peace, with cheerfulness and good humor. Lighten the cares and chase away the vexation to which men, in their commerce with the world, are unavoidably exposed, by rendering his house pleasant to your husband. Keep at home, let your employments be domestic and your pleasures domestic."* [19]

Some wives may be disturbed that they are forgotten by their husbands once they head for work. They feel neglected, that their husbands care more about their work than their wives. And yet, the book **Pathway of Life** states:

> *"He must often forget her, or be useless to the world (his attention must be on his work); she is most useful to the world by remembering him. From the tumultuous scenes which agitate many of his hours, he returns to the calm scene, where peace awaits him, and happiness is sure to await him; because she is there waiting, whose smile is*

peace, and whose very presence is more than
happiness to his heart." [20]

The wife who makes a home, makes the husband remember
her, and he will be there at every moment his responsibility
allows him to be. A wife who nags and argues drives him
away, if not physically, then emotionally. She may feel
trapped or in bondage, and that he is free and she locked in
the home. How untrue! The following, also from the book
Pathway of Life, is worth reading slowly, and even twice, to
understand it.

> *"Just let a young wife remember that her hus-*
> *band necessarily is under a certain amount of*
> *bondage all day; that his interests compel him to*
> *look pleasant under all circumstances, to offend*
> *none, to say no hasty word, and she will see that*
> *when **he reaches his own fireside, he wants,***
> ***most of all, to have this strain removed,** to be at*
> *ease; but this he cannot be if he is continually*
> *afraid of wounding his wife's sensibilities by for-*
> *getting some outward and visible token of his af-*
> *fection for her. Make a home; beautify and*
> *adorn it; cultivate all heavenly charms within it;*
> *sing sweet songs of love in it; bear your portion*
> *of toil, and pain, and sorrow in it; conduct daily*
> *lessons of strength and patience there; shine like*

a star on the face of the darkest night over it, and
tenderly rear the children it shall give you in it.
*High on a pinnacle, **above** all earthly grandeur,*
all gaudy glitter, all fancied ambitions, set the
home interests. Feed the mind in it; feed the soul
in it; strengthen love, charity, truth, and all holy
and good things within it." [21]

Granted, it must also be stated that today's society is not structured correctly and neighborhoods are not communities at all. This does make it most difficult for those wives to be homemakers. Nevertheless, we must start. **"Today"** is the hour of time. Those wives who begin this proven direction will be **martyrs** because it will be difficult to do that which all society is not doing. It will be like swimming against the tide, but happiness and fulfillment awaits the mother who tries and makes it to her island, her home.

Dear Friend,

*"I have always looked forward to receiving your material, and your last book, <u>How to Change Your Husband</u> was no exception. This book has helped me to reflect upon my marriage of 14 years. I felt particularly drawn to the section written about the most sacred part of the home. Once I was asked, 'To what part of the house would you go if you were **dying**?' I thought, but was reluctant to reply — the answer was 'living room.' So where is this 'living room?' Your book gave me the answer."*

A letter from
Sacramento, California

CHAPTER TWELVE

THE MOST SACRED PART OF THE HOME

It is to be a revered point in the home of the husband and wife. It symbolizes their boardroom in which many decisions of their life will be made, both said and unsaid. It is where their children's roots come from, a place where they become one. It is to be where the mother and father kneel and pray. At night it is sacred holy ground, the trunk, the stump; roots of the family are to spring forth from it. The most sacred place in the home is the bed of the husband and wife.

Twenty-eight hundred years ago, Homer [22] wrote of a beautiful, intelligent, graceful couple, Odysseus and Penelope, and their son. Odysseus goes off to fight the Trojan Wars. After ten years, he set sail for home only to be delayed by a sea god for another ten years. Away for twenty years, Penelope and her son ward off a hundred suitors who want Penelope for her beauty as well as Odysseus' home and lands. She does it by asking them to string Odysseus' bow up, which none can. Finally, disguised as a beggar, Odysseus comes home, identifying himself to his son but not his wife. Penelope recognizes him but does not acknowledge him. She brings forth his bow which he immediately strings and with his son kills all the suitors.

Odysseus stood before Penelope, bathed and dressed, and yet she still could not believe her husband had come back to her. Their son wondered how his mother could so coldly sit opposite him and stare. She still wanted to put him to a supreme test and wondered if he treasured the deep secret that only he and she knew. No doubt also she wanted to be wooed by him. She told the servants to take their bed out of the bed chambers and pile the big bed with fleece rugs and sheets of the purest linen.

Immediately Odysseus went into a flashing rage, saying, *"You are trying me. You know I made our bed out of a giant olive tree, building our bedroom around the olive stump. The old olive trunk grew like a pillar on this building plot. I lined up the stone walls, roof, gave it a doorway and smooth fitting doors. I hewed and shaped the stump from the roots up into bedposts, inlaid them with silver, gold, and ivory. There is our sign. No one can move our bed."* As Penelope heard this, her knees grew trembling and weak, her heart nearly failed her. With eyes brimming with tears, she ran to him, throwing her arms around his neck and kissed him.

The bed is a sacred place. It is the sign, **"the symbol"** of love. As it was Penelope and Odysseus' most treasured secret, so too for all married couples is their bed a place of beginning. It is a place where families begin and until recent times, where children came into this world and where those same parents, who birthed the children, left the world, having lived a long and blessed life. From consummation, to birth, to death, it is holy ground; a place that over a lifetime will see tears, joys, grief, and contentment of many natures. It is the center of the home, the atom around which everything else in the home revolves. Our Lady, through Her actions, amazingly shows this.

In 1988, when Marija first came to America, it was impossible for a visionary to go someplace and stay for three months. Yet, Our Lady had a plan to do just that. In Medjugorje, the visionaries knelt before a crucifix hundreds of times to receive Our Lady. To the visionaries it would disappear and Our Lady would be there before them. When the apparition room was moved, Fr. Slavko gave this crucifix to the friend whom Marija later would be staying with in America. Knowing how sacred and special it was, he first brought it to Marija while still in Medjugorje to pray over it — that it be a great instrument for conversion in our country. Marija, along with himself and several others, prayed over it, and then Marija slowly kissed it. The way in which she did it, so reverently, spoke even deeper to the friend of how special a gift this was. He brought it home where it stayed for months in his living room. Later, it happened that Marija was to come to America to donate a kidney to her brother. The friend returned to Medjugorje to get Marija. Several days later, the day before he was to return home, he called his wife and told her he would be bringing Marija to America the next day. That night his wife had a dream that she was to place the crucifix above their bed. She could not sleep, having a tremendous and overwhelming urge to hang the crucifix above their bed along with a statue of Our Lady. All night something pushed her and would not let her rest. Finally, after several hours of struggling, she gave in to this strange burning desire and hung the crucifix from the apparition room in Medjugorje upon the wall overlooking their bed. She said she did not want it there but could only satisfy the urge by doing so. She had never felt anything like this in her entire life. Fulfilling this powerful urge, she felt satisfied and at peace.

When Marija first arrived, it was thought that the apparitions would take place in a church, but when circumstances arose to make that impossible, the second choice was for them to take place in the couple's home. The husband and wife assumed the apparitions would take place in their living room. Marija, however, went into the bedroom, saw the bed and the crucifix over it, and with a strong clear discernment decisively said this is where the apparitions would take place. The husband and wife looked at each other with the same thought, thinking to themselves, *"This is our last choice for the apparitions."* Nevertheless, the first apparition took place over the bed. It was very clear that it was what Our Lady wanted. From over this bed, this rooted stump, a whole mission sprang forth, a whole community. Our Lady birthed many conversions, which were conceived in grace from these apparitions upon this bed. She spoke beautiful words, giving many graces from upon this bed for the next three months. **The Field**, where many people now come with their intentions, was **"birthed"** from this bed. On one particular day Our Lady said from the bed, **"Tomorrow I will appear outside. I invite the public to come."**

That next day's apparition was on Thanksgiving Day and took place near a large pine tree in a field near the home. Many have come to realize that this special apparition is related to the rebirth of our country. Through the action of Our Lady and the prompting of the Holy Spirit, it has become a place where people now gather yearly to pray for our nation's healing. A hundred thousand people have been praying novenas and are continuing to pray them seven months out of the year, for the last three years[*], for the healing of our land, because of this spot in the Field which was birthed upon this bed. One's thought could be, *"One hundred thousand is a lot of people,"* but compared to a nation of two hundred million, it is nothing. Elisha, one man with faith,

---

[*] This was originally written in 1993. Since then hundreds of thousands have been praying these "Seven Novenas..." for 17 years. Refer to footnote on page vi.

closed the Heavens of rain. Three years later with prayers so fervent, he opened them.

If one individual, Elisha, can close the heavens of rain, how much more can one hundred thousand people, praying in union, together from the heart, do for a nation, and all because the husband and wife submitted. The husband submitted totally to God, the wife to the husband. It all revolves around the husband and wife's submission, centered around their bed,* which was God's will. Yearly the numbers of people praying for our nation's healing grows. How far and how big it becomes depends on God's grace and people's prayers. But it all started with a tiny atom, a simple "yes" to God from a man, his wife's "yes" to him, and this prayer universe continues to grow and expand, all in God's order.

And if the wife said no, would the outcome be the same as with Queen Vashti, in which a whole nation could

---

* The bedroom is open only one day a year (falling between December 8 - 12) for people to go and pray. Many conversions as well as several vocations have been birthed from those visits and many receive a special grace. The mother of one seventeen-year-old girl, who would receive a calling while praying there relates: *"My daughter's vocation blossomed during a visit to the bedroom during the 1994 Dedication. Against her will but to make me happy, my daughter agreed to visit this special bedroom. Six months later, she met my husband and me coming down from the grotto at Caritas in tears of joy, saying that she had been fighting it, but she knew God was calling her. She gave up her dance scholarship to college to pursue this path that was so strong on her heart. When we asked her when did this all begin, she said when she visited the bedroom (where Our Lady appeared for three months) at Caritas. She now has joined Regnum Christi, a lay order of consecrated women founded by the Legionaires of Christ."*

have been lost through her refusal? And could it be through her "yes" that a whole nation could be saved, just as what happened with Queen Esther?

"I have a regular visitor that comes to see me (at the Marian center). Her marriage is struggling, but she is not a working mother. That morning she seemed to be different, she was wearing a new ray of hope. I could see this and told her so. Her answer was your book on the family, asking if I had received one and if I had read it. She said once she started to read it, she couldn't put it down, and she realized the things she was doing wrong as a wife and mother and it became known to her the ways in which she could become a better one. Now I couldn't wait till I got home to read it; and since I have begun, I cannot put it down either.

"My husband and I have raised ten children. I was not a working mom. We were poor most of the time, but we had love and God and we were always there for the children to love them, discipline them and give them direction. I, as a mother, was elated and felt extra-special like I never felt before while reading your book. I never realized so deeply that I really was that privileged; that if I was ordained by God to handle motherhood, I could certainly handle second-rate jobs as well and even be overqualified to be the head of a college or fly an F-14 jet. My dreams were to be a stenographer for the president someday, and even wanted to enter a convent, but God wanted motherhood for me. Taking care of ten children all between the ages of one month through 16 years, managing a household and taking care of a husband, takes far more capability and superior wisdom and intelligence than any job the world offers.

"The sacrifices of motherhood contain many jewels and countless blessings, and I and my husband are so blessed with His gifts…Proof that a mother need not work out of the home. God's rewards are waiting for you right here on earth. Trust me! The rewards for staying home and being a mother and wife never end on this earth, and we will continue to reap them through eternity."

*A letter from
Escanaba, Michigan*

122

CHAPTER THIRTEEN

A GOOD WIFE NOT ONLY BUILDS A SMALL CIVILIZATION; SHE CHANGES NATIONS

If the bed is the center, the atom and most sacred part of the home, then what revolves around it? What the bed gives birth to is the fruit of family — children who gather daily around the **table**. This is the second most important piece of furniture in our homes. Likewise, with the deterioration of society, there is a paralleling of the time spent together as family around the table.

One eighteen-year-old who spent a month in Russia said he loved the people. When asked what the best part of his trip was, he revealed it to be meal time.

"It was beautiful. They would sit and eat and talk for two hours every night. I enjoyed this immensely and could feel the love, joys, stories and I longed for it in my family."

Should anyone be surprised that a mother who spends from one to two hours preparing supper, and that within ten to

fifteen minutes after sitting down, everyone is finished eating
and is dispersed by the TV,* telephone, going out, etc., that she
does not feel appreciated? Many mothers feel used, and
rightfully so, after working so hard cooking and preparing, only
to have her flock gather and be dispersed, as if a bunch of torna-
does came through her kitchen. A mother's meal is her feast for
her husband, as Queen Esther gave a feast, a banquet, for the
king. A wife and mother should realize this and begin to teach
her family the importance of sitting and sharing in this banquet
of the mother's goodness, mercy, and love. The husband should
help, encourage, and maintain this nightly feast as a sacred time
with family through his example. Jelena, the innerlocutionist of
Medjugorje, was told by Our Lady on:

December 29, 1984:

**"Today is the <u>feast</u> of the Mother of Goodness,
of Mercy, and of Love."**

Indeed, mealtime is a feast, just as Our Lady's first anniversary celebration of Her coming as "<u>Mother</u> of Goodness,

---

* The TV <u>has</u> no place in the home except that of thief and murderer of the family, both
because of the time it steals from the family and what it promotes, not to mention its deception in the way it delivers its image to you. It is the most singular destructive instrument for killing society. You may obtain a book entitled <u>I See Far</u> explaining its effects on
you and the family from your local bookstore or by writing to **Caritas of Birmingham, 100
Our Lady Queen of Peace Drive, Sterrett, Alabama 35147 USA.** It is highly recommended reading in union with these writings.

Mercy, and Love" in Medjugorje was. While much of a mother's work may be hidden, her preparation for meals is highly visible and takes "goodness" as she must deny herself because she must spend most of her day in planning, organizing and preparing to feed her family for the day. It takes "mercy," when in the middle of the preparation she is interrupted five times to attend to the little ones' hurts and cries. It takes "love" to want the feast to taste good and be enjoyed. Centered around the "table," these attributes of the mother cannot be hidden. They will be seen by the husband, children, and guests who come. While it may not be acknowledged, it will leave an indelible mark on all. It is a statement of the three attributes.

When advertisers want to make a point about motherhood in order to sell something connected to it, they quickly come to show the woman in an apron baking cookies for her children. Though they may be advertising dish detergent to clean the cookie pan with, they know what warms the heart and how to reach the consumer, which, in this case, is a mother, a smile on her face, preparing with goodness the treats she gives with love.

Many healings can take place around the family table. Just because everyone is finished eating shouldn't mean it's time for everyone to get up and that the feast is over. The family is a little kingdom and its feasts should be as in a royal

household. Leaving the table quickly breaks up the kingdom
and weakens it. Staying will strengthen the whole kingdom.

Marija has said that Our Lady told her that reading the
lives of the saints would help us in our lives. One woman,
who was a princess and wanted to enter a cloister, would
change a whole nation and influence all of Europe through
the bed first and then the table. Margaret [23] was in the English court. Born in Hungary in 1047 A.D., she was expected
to live a cultured life. Traveling by ship off the Scottish coast,
a violent storm wrecked their ship. The cast-a-ways were rescued by the illiterate, but powerful, King Malcolm. Rough
and uncouth, his residence reflected the same. It was a drastic
change for Margaret and was little better than a hunting lodge
with little comfort. There were no lovely tapestries to shut
out the drafts or soften the harsh stone walls. Meals were a
disgrace, with food slapped on plates, men coming and going,
carrying on business regardless of whether the king and his
supposedly royal guests were finished eating. The women of
Scotland were similar, as well as the whole country — wild
and uncivilized. As if in a novel, the king asked the beautiful
shipwrecked princess to be his queen. She declined, of
course, telling him she was to be a nun. He insisted and became aggressive. He went to her brother, Egar, who had also
been shipwrecked and very shrewdly explained to him that it
would befit one to cooperate with one's host. Egar, who was
not very brave, immediately urged Margaret to choose mar-

riage over the cloister. She felt, under the circumstances, it was God's will and that this would be the decision she would accept and make the best of it with no regret. Although the illiterate king, his surroundings, home, people, and lands were completely alien to her, she married him. From the bed came forth children and, as queen, she immediately began to change things, around the table in particular. The king had a castle built for her. Margaret set about furnishing it in such a way that it would increase the honor and dignity of those in the court. She purchased gold and silver vessels for eating at the table. She instituted the basic elements of court ceremonial, and to keep the nobles from eating and running, Margaret invented the practice of the Blessing cup. *"Won't you stay to drink the blessing with me?"* she would ask ever so sweetly. Abashed, the hasty men would stay put until the end of the meal.

Her example was not lost on the other women at court, and this civilizing influence gradually spread down through society. A world of cleanliness, health, personal care and beauty, and comfort opened up an exciting vista of hope and new goals for the Scots. As a result, women in particular began to experience a new sense of self-respect and a healthy dose of pride in their appearance and moral standard. [24]

It was not only from the marriage bed that Margaret changed all of Scotland, but also from around the table through her womanly art of homemaking, and with it brought her country out of the backwaters of culture and into mainstream Europe. Trade increased, the church and education grew, and while the king consolidated his divided warring nation, **"Saint"** Margaret of Scotland civilized it, all by obedience to God's plans and structure. A historian, writing in the 19th century, called Margaret the "mirror of wives, mothers, and queens." In her we can see how the gift of motherhood can be extended to a whole people without neglecting one's children.

Indeed, in reading the lives of the women saints, all displayed the same pattern of serving their husbands and living for them. Blessed Anna Maria Taigi, known as "wife, mother, and mystic," died in 1837. Her life was a testimony to serving her husband, family, and strangers. Her desire was so strong to serve that her husband Domenico once asked her when eating:

> *"'Why not sit down and make yourself at ease?'*
> *Whereby she responded, 'Well, Domenico, when*
> *the prince takes his meal does not the servant*
> *stand ready to serve him? Did I not become*
> *your servant from the day you took me as your*
> *wife?"* [25]

If the saints, particularly wives and mothers, were declared so by the Church because they lived right, and all these women saints have this similar pattern of submission to their husbands, then how can it be reconciled that society teaches and encourages women today that they need not be submissive? The Church, by declaring these two mentioned and many other mothers as saints, is in sharp contrast with society. To accept now what society promotes as the "1990's mother," "women coming of age," "doing your own thing" as truths places the Church in untruth. There is no gray line here, and too many for too long have compromised motherhood, all to the detriment and the loss of dignity of women.

The preceding paragraph mutes all arguments anyone could present against submission. The preceding paragraph mutes all arguments anyone could present against submission, for the one who argues against submission, but at the same time, maintains the Church is built on truth, should be reduced to silence by simple logic. And yet, there are those who will argue against submission, and still maintain the Church is built on truth. This is an absurdity that is without logic. We who accept and are swayed by their opinion are greater fools than the ones who boldly state such a contradicting view.

"I always thought I was doing all I could to make my marriage work. I guess it turns out 'all I could' was directed towards the wrong things sometimes, and I have begun to change that direction.

"I knew after reading this book that pointing my finger at my husband's anger and abusive ways is not the way to solve a problem. I need to be a lot more patient and respectful of his wishes, and maybe his anger will not flare up as much.

"This is a very simple way to express the deep feelings and new understanding I have of problems in my marriage. Being at home with a broken ankle and completely dependent on my husband for over a month has given me a crash course in what works and what doesn't work in creating a peaceful environment for us. I have never been dependent on anyone, and I have been on the run for so long that I never took the time to understand the effect of my actions on my husband. I have always been this way.

"Your book has given me some very basic ways to change <u>my</u> ways which I already see are having an effect on my husband."

A letter from
New York

CHAPTER FOURTEEN

WIFEHOOD — MOTHERHOOD
A CALL TO SANCTITY WHICH GIVES BIRTH
TO DIGNITY, WORTH AND PURPOSE,
RESULTING IN JOY

Mirjana, one of the Medjugorje visionaries, said Our Lady never once in Her entire life put Herself first! This may be extremely difficult to obtain but, nevertheless, should be the goal of every wife and mother in her every action. Our Lady knows our hardships, especially those of mothers and wives, and although She is in Heaven, She is still actively our mother and pleads with us to allow Her to help us with all our problems and hardships, as all mothers are supposed to do.

March 2, 1990

> **"Dear children, tonight your Mother asks and pleads: Abandon to me all your problems, all your hardships. I want to prepare you for the day that comes free from all your problems. Give me all your problems."**

Today, indeed, there are many problems. We must go
to the core for the remedy. We must go to the first problem,
which is woman's lack of submission. To bring healing, this
must be reversed. We are in a time which parallels the remedy God first gave to the world over 2000 years ago with a
woman who devoted Her life to complete submission to God,
the Father. It is Our Lady **"today"** who is coming to bring
women back to true dignity, purpose and fulfillment. While
wives and mothers in today's society will have great difficulties going against society and living the Gospels, it still is to be
done. The great joy is knowing Our Lady is actively here to
help. While wives should make every effort to put themselves
second, it should be the husbands who make every effort not
to make that position a burden or an unnecessary hardship.
By the wife being second, the husband should have an honest
desire that she not be so, but rather his helpmate. Her declin-
ing her husband's offer for ease increases his wishes to give
her everything, as Domenico wished for his wife, Blessed Taigi, and she declined. St. Frances De Sales said in his book,
Introduction to the Devout Life:

> *"Husbands, preserve a tender, constant, and*
> *heartfelt love for your wives; the woman was tak-*
> *en from that side which was nearest Adam's*
> *heart, that she might be the more heartily and*
> *tenderly loved. The weakness and infirmities of*
> *your wife, whether mental or bodily, should not*

excite your contempt, but rather a tender loving
compassion; since God has created woman to be
dependent on you, and to add to your honor and
esteem, and although she is given to be your
companion, you are still her head and her supe-
rior. Wives, love the husbands God has given
you, tenderly, heartily, but with a respectful love
and full of reverence; for it is God's will to make
them the superior and more vigorous sex, and He
has ordained that woman would be dependent
upon man, bone of his bone, flesh of his flesh,
taking her from his ribs and beneath his arm, to
show that she is to be subject to the hand of her
husband. And Holy Scripture forcibly inculcates
this subjection, at the same time making it light to
bear, not only bidding you bear the yoke in love,
but also bidding husbands to use their power
gently and lovingly. St. Peter says, 'Ye husbands,
likewise dwelling with them according to know-
ledge, giving honor to the female as to the weaker
vessel.'" [26]

St. Frances De Sales gives examples of husbands and
wives and the drawing forth of the goodness of both.

"There are some fruits, such as the quince, which
are uneatable except when preserved, owing to

their bitterness, and others, such as the apricot
and cherry, which are so delicate that they cannot
be kept except they are preserved. So wives
should endeavor to soften their husbands with
the sugar of devotion, for without it man is but a
rough, harsh being; and husbands should en-
courage their wives in devotion, for without it a
woman is weak and frail. St. Paul says that 'the
unbelieving husband is sanctified by the believ-
ing wife, and the unbelieving wife is sanctified by
the believing husband.' Because in the close un-
ion of matrimony, one may guide the other to
virtue. But that is a truly blessed state in which
the faithful husband and wife sanctify one anoth-
er in the sincere fear of the Lord.

"This mutual support should be such as never to
admit of anger, dissension, or hasty words. Bees
cannot dwell where an echo or other loud noise
prevails; neither will the Holy Spirit abide in that
house which is disturbed by strife, altercation,
and noisy discussions. [27]

A man will not be able to maintain peace which the
wife does not first bring into the home. Only by her creating
peace, which comes from God through order, will there be
something for him to govern. If she makes the loud noise of

nagging and war, nothing he can do will bring peace. The following parable shows it is the wife who is the first generator for peace or war.

Two women who were neighbors had wells in the back of their yards from which they drew forth their water. The wells were identical, with dirt and clay sides and were the same depth because of the water table being the same over the whole area. When the two women first began using the wells, they clumsily clanked and dropped the buckets into the well, stirring up the sediment which brought forth cloudy water. Day by day, the women went out, all the while one of the women grew more and more angry over the cloudy water in the well. As each day passed, she became rougher, dropping the bucket, hitting the side walls, cracking off dirt, soiling the water further. She soon despised the well. Her anger grew each day so much that soon she only drew a half a pail of water, splashing the other half out. She mumbled to and fro all the while only to drag the bucket the next day on the ground, kicking and complaining until soon dents covered the bucket. Soon rust followed and holes appeared, only allowing one-fourth of a bucket of dirty water to be drawn forth from the well.

The second woman of a sweeter, gentler disposi-
tion noticed the cloudy water and day after day
thought to herself, "If I lower the bucket slower
and a little more gently, perhaps the water will be-
come more clear." Indeed, she learned the way of
patience and began to draw forth crystal clear
sweet water. Day by day, she learned to love going
to the well and looked forward to the cool refresh-
ment it offered her. Even years later, her seasoned
bucket brought forth full buckets of the well water.
She felt so blessed to be given such a good well,
while the other woman felt cursed to be given such
a bad well, yet both were identical wells.

As St. Frances De Sales says, men are but rough, harsh
beings. The well and bucket represent the husband. The
cloudy water in the beginning is the man in the rough. The
first woman, first marrying her husband, sees his rough harshness (cloudy water). Her response can make him soften or
become harsher. The first woman's nagging draws forth from
him harsher treatment of her, just as the well drew forth dirtier and dirtier water. Her demanding, warring, rebellious
behavior is met with the same treatment back to her, even
worse, as he is already a harsh being. But it is she who by her
disposition draws forth her husband's wrath, as it was the
woman's fault in drawing forth the filthy water. She becomes
further disenchanted, not receiving any love, etc. from him, so

that she soon despises him. He, tired and beat, develops a harshness and insensitivity towards her, and she doesn't comprehend why. His response to loving her deteriorates to very little, just as eventually she could draw only a quarter of a bucket of water. He soon even dreads to go home and finds reasons to stay away.

The second woman represents a wife who, marrying her husband, finds him also rough and harsh, just as the second woman's well water was cloudy. The wife is a little confused in the beginning, but reasons out that if she responds back to him harshly, he will become harsher since that is his nature. Instead she chooses to remain patient and gentle. She decides steadfastly on a sweet disposition. Just as the second woman began to draw forth cleaner and cleaner water from the well, so too the wife draws forth the good out of her husband. The second woman grew more and more satisfied with the well and longed to arrive at it to feel and taste the cool fresh water. Just as she, who over time, changes and civilizes her husband and in turn longs for the joy of their meeting at the end of the day. She is grateful that she has a good husband who loves, provides, and shelters her. And so, though the wells were identical, reflecting the husbands of the two, the second woman felt so blessed by having a good husband, the same as she felt towards the good well; yet the first woman felt cursed by having what she believed was a bad husband as well as a bad well.

"My wife never respected me as her husband and made life very hard for me. When I was out of work I had job offers out of town, but she would not leave her mother. She told me if I went I would go alone. She viewed children more as a hindrance than a gift from God. Maybe it is a blessing we didn't have children to grow up in this kind of environment. She nagged at me and embarrassed me in public in front of my friends and family. When I lost one job I had, she chastised me instead of supporting me. After awhile all this works on your self-esteem. She took away my manhood. She told me on more than one occasion that 'I was crazy' if I thought she was going to wait on me hand and foot the way your mom does with your dad.

"I have a close friend who has five children and a loving wife. They are the perfect example of a loving Christian couple. His wife lets him lead the family. She respects and is submissive to him. They are both very happy. He loves his wife and family more than anything. If I tell my wife to look at them as an example she becomes angry. If I thought she was going to be like that then I had another thing coming."

A letter from
Altoona, Pennsylvania

CHAPTER FIFTEEN

MODERN SOCIETY'S IDEAS OF WIFEHOOD AND MOTHERHOOD, OF EQUAL AUTHORITY, AND SELF-INTEREST GIVE BIRTH TO LACKOF DIGNITY, LITTLE WORTH, AND LITTLE PURPOSE, RESULTING IN DEPRESSION

Today many women are "dissatisfied" with who they are, while men don't seem to "know" who they are. Bombarded with magazines such as *Cosmopolitan, Self,* etc. promoting self-interest, it is no wonder women have suffered the loss of much self esteem, as well as respect in society. In every billboard, every magazine ad, TV commercial, etc., women are displayed as little better than prostitutes. While men with unchecked passions may pretend they like that, they will never respect it, and it is one major factor which has led to more abuses to women. Examples are everywhere. Just look at what any of the high school, even in Christian and Catholic high schools, cheerleaders do. Their body movements are totally without dignity and virtue and, sadly, usually all this is under the watchful eye of a grownup who has the title of <u>mother</u> and who condones these actions.

The power of women is so great that when they are good and virtuous, there is no sweetness that surpasses them, but when rebellious, there is no war that can equal their wrath. We talk a lot about many fathers abandoning their wives and children. Man has within his make-up an innate desire to protect and to provide. It may anger and surprise many, but most husbands and fathers do not set out to abandon their families, nor do they want to. The largest contributing factor over and over to men abandoning their homes is that the wife hasn't made it a home. No man will long to dwell where there is disobedience, no peace, and no respect. Scripture has it:

Proverbs 21:19

> *"It is better to dwell in a wilderness than with*
> *a quarrelsome and vexatious wife."*

Ray Mossholder, an extremely successful marriage counselor and pastor who literally stops divorces wherever he goes, says **a man will not change that which he doesn't think he can.** A wife, who constantly disrupts or compromises a husband's guidance, will in many cases eventually drive him away. Realizing there is no use for him to try bringing about change because she blocks it, he eventually falls into complacency, is henpecked, or leaves.

Aristotle's quote: *"A man is in his house to rule, not be ruled over,"* is supported by the Bible.

Sirach 9:2

"Give no women power over you to trample upon your dignity."

It is very difficult for a man to stay around and want to please his wife once she has done this. It is in the hands of the woman to lift up all of mankind or bring it down, just as Eve sinned and usurped Adam's command not to eat the fruit, the command which he received from the Father. She disobeyed her husband and instead of following her husband, she followed her own wants for things. Ivan, the visionary, has already been quoted as saying that many women force their husbands into complacency to get the things they want.

Eve was attracted to a thing and desired it more than obedience to her husband and through him to the Father. If Adam had stood up to her perhaps the human race could have been salvaged, but he did not. He came under the rule of the woman, attracted and seduced by her.

Sirach 25:23

"In woman is sin's beginning and because of her we all die."

St. Paul, however, says it is Adam as head of the race that we receive "Original Sin" and its punishments. Any time man reverses his God-ordained role, he places the wife in a position of guiding, and its fruit **will** result in a deterioration of society. While no one wants to admit it, we currently have a society guided heavily by female influence and domination. It does not mean a woman cannot guide. She must be able to do so to run a home, to help with her husband's lands, to assist him in his enterprises, etc., but only by working in union with him through his guidance, through his consenting and through his delegating, and when there are differences, through her will coming into union with his.

Adam was to follow God and Eve was to follow Adam. Eve reversed that and followed the demon. Adam, in turn, followed Eve. This reversal of authority, as all know, had devastating consequences, and is the central core of the problem today in society where the center cannot hold. Wives without husbands as their guide are apt to go astray. Elizabeth Rice Handford in her book, Your Clothes Say It For You, put it this way:

"First Timothy 2:13,14 tells us, 'For Adam was first formed, then Eve. And Adam was not deceived, but the woman being deceived was in the transgression.' Eve actually believed the lie satan told her about the fruit of the tree of knowledge of good and evil. Adam knew satan lied, but he ate anyway. Why? There was, of course, the element of rebellion against God.

"Ever since that fateful day, the woman has been the less spiritually discerning. We usually think of women being more spiritually minded than men. After all, the average church has many more women than men in its services. Too, women probably talk more about their spiritual concerns than men do.

"But the sad truth is, women are more easily led into sin than men are. They more quickly accept heresy. Think of the large number of cults that were founded by women. The numerical ratio of women to men in cult leadership perhaps surpasses that of any other field. They can easily 'wax wanton against Christ' and have 'damnation' because they have cast off their first faith, as I Timothy 5:11 and 12 says. False teachers will 'creep into houses, and lead captive silly women

*laden with sins, led away with diverse lust, ever
learning, and never able to come to the knowledge of the truth' (II Tim. 3.6,7). First Peter 3:7
calls a woman 'the weaker vessel,' referring perhaps as much to her spiritual frailties as to her
body.*

*"But God has made a marvelous provision for a
woman, and that is the loving, wise, compassio-
nate protection of her husband. If she will submit herself to her husband, then she is safe from
the most virulent of satan's attacks.*

*"Ruth the Moabite said to her kinsman Boaz,
'Spread therefore thy skirt over thine handmaid;
for thou art a near kinsman' (Ruth 3:9). She was
asking him to be her husband, to protect her
physically, spiritually, and emotionally. When
Naomi broached the question of a husband for
her widowed daughter-in-law, she asked 'Shall I
not seek rest for thee, that it may be well with
thee?' Rest would come to Ruth in the arms of
Boaz, covered by the skirt of his protection.*

*"We read the parable in Ezekiel 16 of the God-
man who rescued the baby girl from death.
Verse 8 says, 'Now when I passed thee, and*

*looked upon thee, behold, thy time was the time
of love; and I spread my skirt over thee, and covered thy nakedness: yea, I swear unto thee, and
entered into a covenant with thee, saith the Lord
God, and thou becamest mine.' The bride had
heart-wrenching needs. Her Bridegroom met
them all, and committed Himself forever to continue meeting them.*

*"This covering and protection means blessing
and comfort to the wife, not deprivation or
abuse. (To hear us wives complain of it would
make you think the opposite — that God had not
intended it for our good.) King Solomon's bride
said of her husband, 'I sat down under his shadow with great delight, and his fruit was sweet to
my taste. He brought me to the banqueting
house, and his banner over me was love' (Song
of Sol. 2:3,4). The Hebrew word 'shadow' is also
translated 'defence.' This bride felt secure under
the shadow, the defence of her husband. And
notice the banner: his banner, his protection, was
not duty, not lordship, but love! He loved her!
How a wife ought to welcome her husband's protection. She receives it by submitting to him.*

"...the husband's protection for his wife is a kind of 'blinders.' Blinders keep a horse from seeing frightening movements or distractions on the side, and shying at them. So a woman's submission to her husband can keep her single-minded, oblivious to the temptations that might flaunt themselves before the rebellious wife."[28]

*An article published by **Inside the Vatican** stated:*

*"The devil prefers to take possession of women, according to the official exorcist for the diocese of Rome, **Father Gabriele Amorth**. 'It is above all women who are stricken by the demonic because they are more easily exposed than men to the danger of the demonic,' Amorth told an interviewer. 'I have encountered numerous cases of women who, because of demonic possession, were forced to prostitute themselves. For this reason, they have no moral blame.' Amorth has conducted hundreds of exorcisms in Rome over the past 20 years.*

"'The women preyed upon by satan are especially those who are young and of pleasing appearance,' the exorcist said. 'During some exorcisms, the demon, with a terrifying voice, has roared that he seeks to enter women rather than men in order to take revenge on the Madonna because he has been humiliated by Mary.'

"Amorth said he is extremely worried by the rapid rise of occult practices among Italian young people in recent years. His remarks were published in 'La Stampa' on December 11, 1995."

CHAPTER SIXTEEN

WHY IS IT IMPORTANT THAT WIVES SUBMIT TO THEIR HUSBANDS?

The Church has always taught the importance of spiritual direction and its effect for the good of the soul on those who are under the spiritual director. A husband is under the direction of God the Father in "aspects" as to the decisions of what is best for his wife and family. His wife is under his direction. When this is not in order, as mostly is the case during this age, women can lose their identity and become little more than instruments of men. This has lead to a great amount of evil in society, just as Eve birthed it in the beginning with her forsaking her husband and thereby God.

As already stated, nothing is better than a sweet, gentle, and loving mother, and nothing is more evil than a rebellious, wicked, and worthless one, even if beautiful.

Proverbs 11:22

> *"Like a golden ring in a swine's snout is a beautiful woman with a rebellious disposition."*

The same juvenile probation officer[29] previously quoted twice said that the juvenile girls they bring in to detention are far worse than the boys. He said, in most cases, they have to be cuffed to the bed. They are wild. Another probation officer, who was a **female** said, *"You give me five juvenile boys to take care of any day as opposed to one juvenile girl!"*

One father relates how he saw two girls fighting in high school and even though he had seen several guys fight, he had never seen viciousness compared to what the two girls did to each other.

The **<u>Poem of the Man-God</u>** is a book, contained in five volumes, that was written in the 1940's by Maria Valtorta. It gives excellent spiritual direction and is based on alleged visions she had of Christ and the apostles. Recently its popularity has caused so much attention and respect for the book that Marija, the visionary, was asked to ask Our Lady about this book — if we were able to read it. This was asked because there are real enemies to the book, and they oppose the book fiercely, even condemning anyone who reads it. So the question was put to Our Lady and She answered, affirming that it could be read and added that it would be good to read it. The fact that Our Lady answered at all is a very strong endorsement of the book. The Church has recently ruled — <u>Yes, the faithful may read them, but not to proclaim them as supernatural in origin.</u> This move by the Church is a reflection of all its past history in how it confirms saints, miracles, writings, etc., which is with time, allowing exposure or devotion to it, all the time watching its fruits, thereby having something in the future to judge by.

There is a scene in the fourth volume where Jesus just performed an exorcism on a woman and the apostle Matthew questions Jesus about why so many more possessions are of women than of men.

> *"Matthew: Why, Master do we notice that many women are possessed by the demon, and we can say, by that demon (the demon of want, desire)?*

> *"Jesus answers: Matthew, woman is not equal to man in her formation and in her reaction to the original sin. Man has other aims for his desires which may be more or less good. Woman has one aim only: love. Man has a different formation. Woman has this one, sensitive, which is even more perfect, because its purpose is procreation. You know that every perfection brings about an increase in sensitiveness. A perfect ear can hear what escapes a less perfect ear and is glad of that. The same applies to the eyes, to the palate and to olfaction. Woman was to be the sweetness of God on the Earth, she was to be*

love, the incarnation of that fire which moves Him Who is, the manifestation, the testimony of that love. God had therefore gifted her with a super eminent sensitive spirit, so that, one day as a mother, she could and would know how to open the eyes of the hearts of her sons to the love for God and their fellow-creatures, as man would open the eyes of intelligence of his children to understanding and acting. Consider the command of God to Himself: 'Let us make a helpmate for Adam.' God — Goodness could but want to make a good helpmate for Adam. He who is good loves. Adam's helpmate, therefore, was to be able to love to succeed in making Adam's day happy in the blissful Garden. She was to be so capable of loving <u>as to be the second collaborator and substitute of God, in loving man,</u> His creature, so that even when God did not reveal Himself to His child with His loving voice, man should not feel unhappy for lack of love. satan was aware of such perfection. satan knows so many things. It is he who speaks through the lips of pythonesses (in the garden) telling lies mixed with truth. And — <u>bear this in mind</u> all of you, both you who are present here and those who will come in future — <u>he speaks</u>

such truth, which he hates because he is False-
hood, only to seduce you with the chimera that it
is Light that speaks and not Darkness. satan,
cunning, tortuous and cruel, crept into such per-
fection, he bit there and left his poison. The per-
fection of woman in loving has thus become sa-
tan's instrument to dominate man and woman
and spread evil...

"John the apostle asks: What about our mothers,
then?

"Jesus answers: John, do you fear for them?
Not every woman is an instrument for satan.
Perfect as they are in their feelings, they exceed in
action: angels if they want to be of God, demons
if they wish to be of satan. Holy women, and
your mother is one of them, want to be of God
and they are angels.

"John: Do You not think that the punishment of
woman is unfair, Master? Man also sinned.

"Jesus: And what about the reward then? It is
written that Good will come back to the world
through Woman and satan will be defeated.
Never judge the work of God. That is the first

thing. But consider that as Evil came into the world through woman, it is fair that through the Woman Good should come into the world. A page written by satan is to be cancelled. And the tears of a Woman will do that. And as satan will shout his cries for ever, the voice of a Woman will sing to drown those cries." [30]

Indeed Our Lady is coming to do just that. Her singling out wives and mothers for Her Motherly Blessing is confirmation that through mothers, life will re-enter the world. Ivanka was told by Our Lady after she had just given birth to a child:

June 25, 1990

"I thank you for giving your life to allow other life."

In regard to the just wife, the good woman, Jesus is asked in the **Poem of the Man-God** about man's incoherence. A woman named Johanna says:

"Master! I was almost certain. Now I am completely sure. The incoherence of men is really great! Their attachment to interests is very strong! And their pity for their wives is really so faint! We are... Even we, the wives of the best husbands, what are we? A jewel which is dis-

played or concealed according to its useful-
ness...A mime who must laugh or weep, attract
or reject, speak or be silent, show or hide herself
in compliance with her man's wishes... always in
his interest... Our destiny is a sad one, Lord!
And degrading as well!

"Jesus responds: As compensation your spirits
are enabled to climb higher." [31]

In giving more instructions to wives and mothers, Maria Valtorta writes that Jesus says:

"The wife at home must be just with her hus-
band, her children, and servants. She must obey,
respect, console and help her husband. She is to
be obedient, providing her obedience does not
imply consent to sin. The wife must be submis-
sive but not degraded. Beware, O wives, that the
first to judge you, after God, for certain guilty
condescension, are your very husbands, who
persuade you to comply. They are not always
desires of love, but they are also tests for your
virtue. Even if he does not think about it at the
moment, the day may come when the husband
may say to himself: 'My wife is very sensual' and
thence he may begin to be suspicious of her fidel-

*ity. Be chaste in your conjugality. Behave in
such a way that your chastity may impose on
your husband that reservedness which one has
for pure things, and they may consider you their
equals, not as slaves or concubines kept only for
'pleasure' and rejected when they are no longer
liked. The virtuous wife, I would say the wife
who also after conjugality retains that virginal
'something' in attitude, in words, in her trans-
ports of love, can lead her husband to an elevation from sensuality to sentiment, whereby the
husband divests himself of lewdness and becomes really 'one thing' with his wife, whom he
treats with the same respect with which a man
treats a part of himself, which is just, because the
wife is 'bone from his bones and flesh from his
flesh' and no man ill-treats his bones or his flesh,
on the contrary he loves them, and therefore
husband and wife, like the first married couple,
look at each other without seeing their sexual nakedness, but let them love each other because of
their spirits, without degrading shame.*

*"Let the wife be patient and motherly with her
husband. Let her consider him as the <u>first of her</u>
children, because a woman is always a mother
and man is always in need of a patient, prudent,*

affectionate, comforting mother. Blessed is the woman who knows how to be the companion and at the same time the mother of her husband to support him, and his daughter to be guided by him. A wife must be industrious. "[32]

Dear Caritas,

"I remember growing up how my mother always came to our defense if our father ever corrected or disciplined us. She always had a reason for our behavior — 'They're only' — 'We did' — 'I should have' — 'You shouldn't have' — 'You can't expect', etc. Always the responsibility was lifted from us. As a result we were never able to accept the responsibilities of our actions. It was easy to always make an excuse for ourselves — 'If the vase hadn't been so close to the edge, who put it there?' — 'If she hadn't made me so upset I..,' etc. I believe my father just gave up. His authority was taken away. After all, what my mother did always seem to be right or logical. We went undisciplined. Not that we became such terrible children — we weren't the worst or the best — but it wasn't just the vase being broken we found an excuse for, but sin. It was never our fault. This, of course, carried into our teens (you can imagine what we were like) and through as adults. Once my sister was visiting and she opened the oven to take out the dinner I had prepared. She grasped the pot with her bare hands, burning herself. The dinner went all over the floor. She immediately said, 'What is this kind of pot doing in the oven?' It was a type of casserole for stove top or oven. I immediately saw myself and what my husband had been trying to tell me for so many years.

"I also saw how I would do this in the raising of my own children. It is still so difficult for me to discipline them as my first reaction is the why's and reasons they behaved this way — the excuse. In my mind, the poor child is just a victim of circumstance — 'If only I…' — 'They wouldn't have if…', etc. I am torn because I know what is right, but this is so deep within me. It is difficult to change even when you want to. It has been difficult for my husband, too, as he has had to be so much stronger with our children to compensate for my weakness. It has created many problems in our marriage. Please pray for me. I see from your book <u>How to Change Your Husband</u> more and more my failings, yet as I said, even when you want to change it is difficult because of the way you are raised is so deep within you (another excuse?).

"I can see in society how prevalent this is — the court system, for instance, the offender or criminal is treated as a victim, the victim torn apart as the accuser. This world we live in today really needs the guidance of a good mother, our Mother Mary.

"Please send me four copies of your book. I want to give them to my brothers and sisters. Thank you!"

Eugene, Oregon

CHAPTER SEVENTEEN

WHEN A MOTHER PUTS HER CHILDREN EQUAL OR ABOVE THE HUSBAND, SOCIETY DETERIORATES

The husband is to be placed above the children by the wife. He is to take first place. This action is a statement of respect and love and will increase when the children see the mother's love go first to the husband rather than first to the children. Rather than the children feeling deprived, they will feel secure. Insecurity will come to the children when the children's place in the home is elevated equal or above that of the father. Fr. Paul Wickens says it is inordinate of the wife when this happens. He goes on further, saying:

> *"Excessive possessiveness on the part of a mother can violate these vows (the husband and wife are one mind, one in heart, one in affection) by placing the children <u>before</u> her husband in terms of affection. The husband should <u>not be in second place</u>, either in affection from his wife or in love from his children."* [33]

The father, being in the first position, then becomes supreme in the eyes of his children and society benefits. Respect for all positions follows suit from the fireman to the school teacher.

A father's "right" in leading his family is **supreme**, that of his wife supreme also — second <u>only</u> to the husband's. The shepherd of the family is the father. **<u>No one</u>** has a right to contradict his guidance (unless he is leading them to sin). The father's right to guide, if contradicted, will most definitely lead to a deterioration of family order. He directs the wife and children. It doesn't mean a wife cannot have a spiritual director, but if his direction (the spiritual director) goes against the husband about issues then she is to drop the spiritual director (issues meaning the father's direction on attitudes, family plans, etc...or standards he desires from his wife and children, etc.). One wife, who went for direction from a priest, received direction concerning issues of which the priest had no right to contradict the father in, since they were not of an immoral nature. This bad spiritual direction escalated a war and prolonged terrible suffering and destruction within the family. The priest had no biblical basis to direct the wife or give her support in her position contrary to the direction of the husband and father. The issues involved were placed by the priest's spiritual direction above the God-ordained structure of the husband, which birthed very bad fruit for an extended period of time. Sadly, and perhaps shamefully to those many Catholics who advise such, it was a Protestant minister who helped the wife rise above the issues to follow God's structure and walk with the husband. Healing began after over three years of war. Peace, order, and love are coming into the home through the father to the mother, then to the children. Currently there are <u>great violations</u> to the natural order. These violations are coming through destructive teachings from the pulpit all throughout society. It is a violation to solid marriages and order. A simple statement from the above priest directing the wife, saying, *"Do as your husband says, it is Scriptural; this is your path and key to happiness,"* would have avoided many tragedies. Yet in the spirit of compromising God's words, the advice is always **"compromise"** — a word which is found nowhere in the Scriptures and is actually more related to the relaxing of the spiritual life in that it is always on the main agenda of satan to "compromise." When God the Father clearly shows a father in the family what to do, and the wife wishes to compromise it, woe to him who gives in — double woe to him who directs and encourages the wife toward her rebellion or who supports it.

It is necessary to be severe here. **While there are many good and holy priests who give good solid direction,** there are also many priests or other directors who betray these sound, proven biblical principles, and they have contributed in a large degree to the divorce and separation we suffer from today. One wife was advised by three different priests to divorce her husband. They all felt after talking to the wife that she was abandoned. In truth, he landed a job which required him to move to another city, which he did. She, not wanting to leave her mother and other considerations, would not follow. The three priests, weak and lacking wisdom, went to the issues of their consideration and sympathized with the wife, which further separated the married couple. If, instead, they would have gone to God's biblical structure for the family and said to the wife, *"You are to follow your husband,"* unity would have resulted.

The tragic reality is that there are many Judases today among the pulpits, giving destructive and devastating advice. There are two directions of advice, two choices one has in trying to bring about peace and harmony in relationships: "settlement of issues" or "God's ordained structure." The "settlement of issues" will require "compromise." God's ordained structure will require the "blending of wills". Sadly, compromise is the advice and choice for most who advise and counsel today. And has divorce and separation decreased as more and more of this advice has been given? Rather it has escalated. Compromise is the direction given because many teachers do not want to advise "submission" as the choice. These teachers are trying to hold society and families together by "compromise." The word itself speaks of its bad fruit when applied to marriage. One of the dictionary meanings of "compromise":

"to **endanger**, to make a **shameful or disreputable concession**." [34]

How is it not only do we not find this word any place in Holy Scripture but also nowhere in Our Lady's messages? Certainly, as much as this is advised world-wide to hold families and marriages together, you would think out of over thousands of words Our Lady has given, there would be at least one reference to it. How can it be reconciled that this is the first conclusion of so many spiritual advisors, counselors, etc...and yet not once does Our Lady say it! Is She not coming to heal the family? Why is She out of tune with the prevailing thought? Is She out of touch with the solution which so many intelligent individuals give?

Compromise many times leads to a decrease in values. One father related:

> *"I wanted to protect the hearts of my children*
> *and what they were exposed to. I did not want*
> *them to be exposed to things which entertained*
> *the breaking of God's precepts. Yet, I was told*
> *by several advisors, even priests, that I must*
> *compromise to help maintain peace in the family.*
> *How can I make compromises to a song which*
> *promotes the loosening of morals? How can I*
> *compromise with what God has shown me and*

let my children watch a sports event in which the commercials promote every vice from lust, to excess want of material goods, to excessive pleasure and living for self? All I heard is, 'You must compromise.' I now see how so many values have been eroded through compromise."

Indeed "compromise" has far more to do with satan than with God. Line up all God's precepts, all His ways, all His truths, all the holy actions of the saints who applied these ways of God. Where out of the millions of actions of charity, love, and goodness can the word "compromise" be applied? Come forward you individuals who hold the title of directors, counselors, advisors, teachers of the Word and show where God wants His laws compromised? Where could even one saint out of the thousands apply it to God's will in his life? Find one place to apply it to His Ten Commandments! You cannot find one, and yet you advise it everyday! Compromise does not bring "harmony." It may, for a time, bring about "quietness" between a couple, but not the joining together of hearts, which is true harmony. Compromise will actually keep them separate as man and woman and wait for the next crisis to further separate them when it arises, just as a monster will devour its prey. Compromise is a word and an action of the world. **Compromise leads to future dissensions. "Harmony" leads to the blending of wills. It is the word to use. It is the goal. Harmony can only exist where there is good solid struc-**

ture. It is the place to begin to solve issues. The harmony of a husband depends on his blending his will to God's, the wife's to the husband's, and the children the same. This, in turn, puts you in harmony with your neighbor, who, if he does the same with his family, makes society become one. You with society will then be before God and in harmony with Him.

The following words show the wisdom of not compromising, even in a simple situation when to compromise would "seem" appropriate:

> *"My wife and I were out with the kids and I was in the mood to eat Bar-B-Que. My wife, in union with my children wanted Mexican food. My wife, using wisdom, said 'No, we will all go and eat Bar-B-Que.' My wife in doing this promoted respect for me and my word as a husband and father, and strengthened my authority. This move of leading herself and the children to meet my needs made the ground fertile for me to show love to my wife and children as Christ loved the Church. For after she told the children the family would eat what I wanted, I was able then to say, 'I'll tell you what! Because I love you all so much, let's go eat Mexican!'*

"My wife could have said, 'Let's compromise,' which would have started a debate and most likely ended in an argument as it deteriorated. She could have said, 'It's five against one,' which would have caused a deterioration of respect, placing my fatherhood on an equal vote as one with the children. She could have made one of a dozen other statements to compromise my role. Instead, she responded in such a way which elevated both her role and my role and peace was the fruit. Any compromise at all would have changed the whole outcome.

"I like for my wife to set up situations such as this because it gives me the opportunity to reciprocate with love. While this is the course I take most of the time, I believe, as a father, children should also learn that the family is not a democracy and that sometimes it is important that they see the action of my wife carried through. So there are occasions where, if all wanted to do one thing and I another that I will go with my suggestion, not because of selfishness but rather because there is great value in teaching children to follow their father, through the witness of their mother joyfully pleasing him. There are few

more effective ways to breed respect, love and joy
in the family."

Therefore, it must be re-established in society to the highest degree that fatherhood and its right to rule cannot be compromised. The father's right is so supreme that even the Pope does not have the right to usurp it (except in sin), nor will Christ Himself contradict it. The father is accountable to God and heavy will be his load for ignoring the divine prompting he as a father <u>will</u> receive from God the Father to guide his family. Again in the Poem of the Man-God, Jesus says:

"But woe to fathers who fail in their duties, who
are blind and deaf to the need and faults of the
members of his family." [35]

A wife may think, *"But I'm right about a certain issue!"* It is very important to note that **obedience is more important than being right.** How many of the saints, so many times, were in the right and their superiors wrong, yet they always were joyfully obedient. The children may sometimes see that their father may not be perfectly right in a certain circumstance, but through the wife and her example they will learn that they still must obey. It will teach them (the children) to obey a teacher, a policeman, the government, etc. when it is not perfectly right. Order can still be maintained even in the midst of imperfections. The children will comply when they grow up if they were shown through example to respect and be obedient. Therefore, respect and obedience will be maintained even where there are imperfections which will be found in every government, every institution, and every family. But even if there were perfection, order will not be maintained where there is disrespect and disobedience, and anarchy will ensue. It is worth repeating - **obedience is more important than being right.** Of course, love has to be its foundation to produce good fruit. However, even if love is not found, there still can be no excuse not to obey.

"Even though humanly speaking I do not like the fact that God put men in charge, through grace, I believe in my heart that such is the way God designed it and consequently I must accept it. The reason why it's hard for us women to accept this is because it represents a cross, the dying to ourselves, which we all try to escape."

> *A letter from*
> *Alexandria, Virginia*

CHAPTER EIGHTEEN

BUT MY HUSBAND IS NOT AS SMART AS ME ABOUT THINGS

OK, if obedience is more important than being right, what if a husband wants to take their life's savings to invest and the wife's wisdom tells her it will be a mistake and she knows she is right? She must be obedient, even if because of his decision they lose their home, cars, everything. The family order will still be intact. That is far better fruit than rebellion against the husband bringing rebellion into the family, thereby killing it in the war which could result. What good will the house be, the cars, etc.? You can recover from a dumb idea, but the devastation of family is far more difficult to heal. Holding the family together, however, does not mean for the wife to say, *"I was against it. I let you do it and look what happened! You should have listened to me!"* These are bitter statements which will infect your children. Ray Mossholder says:

> *"Bitterness, like acid, destroys the container it is stored in."*

One wife, who literally made her husband what he is today, a great pastor in California, not only followed him in his mistakes but **encouraged** him along once he decided for them, even though it was against her better judgement! It is an incredible testimony of a wife, and after reading it you will agree she is a saint, not so much symbolically as in reality. What you are about to read was told by the husband, E.V. Hill, of his wife Jane, who was near him when he gave this message. James Dobson, the founder of "Focus on the Family," recalls this message he heard and says that it was one of the most moving messages he had ever heard from anyone. E.V. states:

> *"As a struggling young preacher, I had trouble earning a living. That led me to invest the family's scarce resources, over Jane, my wife's, objections, in the purchase of a service station. She felt I lacked the time and expertise to oversee this investment, which proved to be accurate. Eventually, the station went broke and we lost our shirts in the deal.*

> *"It was a critical time in my life as a young man. I had failed at something important and my wife would have been justified in saying, 'I told you so.' But Jane had an intuitive understanding of my*

vulnerability. Thus, when I called to tell her that I had lost the station, she said simply, 'All right.'

"I came home that night expecting my wife to be pouting over my foolish investment. Instead, she sat down with me and said, 'I've been doing some figuring. I figure that you don't smoke and you don't drink. If you smoked and drank, you would have lost as much as you lost in the service station. So, it's six in one hand and a half-dozen in the other. Let's forget it.'

"Jane could have shattered my confidence as a husband at that delicate juncture. The male ego is surprisingly fragile, especially during times of failure and embarrassment. That's why I needed to hear her say, 'I still believe in you,' and that is precisely the message she conveyed to me.

"Shortly after the fiasco with the service station, I came home one night and found the house dark. When I opened the door, I saw that my wife had prepared a candlelight dinner for two.

"'What meanest thou this?' I said with characteristic humor.

"'Well,' said Jane, 'we're going to eat by candle-light tonight.'

"I thought that was a great idea and went into the bathroom to wash my hands. I tried unsuccess-fully to turn on the light. Then I felt my way into the bedroom and flipped another switch. Dark-ness prevailed. I went back to the dining room and asked Jane why the electricity was off. She began to cry.

"'You work so hard, and we're trying,' said Jane, 'but it's pretty rough. I didn't have quite enough money to pay the light bill. I didn't want you to know about it, so I thought we would just eat by candlelight.'

"Dr. Hill described his wife's words with intense emotion: 'She could have said, 'I've never been in this situation before. I was reared in the home of Dr. Caruthers, and we never had our lights cut off.' She could have broken my spirit; she could have ruined me; she could have demoralized me. But instead she said, 'Somehow or another we'll get these lights on. But let's eat tonight by candlelight.'

"She was my protector. Some years ago I received quite a few death threats, and one night I received notice that I would be killed the next day. I woke up thankful to be alive. But I noticed that she was gone. I looked out the window and my car was gone. I went outside, and finally, saw her driving up in her robe. I said, 'Where have you been?' She said, 'I...I...it just occurred to me that they could have put a bomb in that car last night, and if you had gotten in there you would have been blown away. So I got up and drove it. It's all right.'"[36]

The above was a strong message. There was not a dry eye in the house and no one doubted that June Hill was a saint. Indeed, she was close to her husband while he delivered this message because it was the eulogy at her funeral, as she lay near him in her coffin. How many lives will be touched by this wonderful woman through her husband? What legacy will you leave as a wife and mother when you are gone? Will your spirit carry on through to your husband and children? If so, what kind of spirit have you deposited there? What is imprinted on your little boys' and girls' hearts .....by your love? or Indifference?....Charity? or Selfishness? .....Kindness? or Meanness?

"My head is simply swimming with all the 'food for thought' in your last book which is more like an epistle to us <u>mothers</u>."

A letter from
Greenwich, Connecticut

CHAPTER NINETEEN

WOMEN POTENTIALLY HAVE TREMENDOUS POWER AND INFLUENCE, YET TODAY THEY ACTUALLY HAVE LITTLE BECAUSE OF THE LOSS OF WISDOM IN HOW TO OBTAIN IT

Every little boy and girl comes through the mother. Her influence is great; and when we see a bad father, can we still not trace it back to who first nursed him? Who was first there with him or not there with him because of selfish wants? Many mothers are annoyed by their children's habits which many times were taught to them by the mothers themselves.

H.B. London is the vice president in charge of Outreach and Pastoral Relations for "Focus On The Family." The following was taken from a question and answer interview about family:

Q: Do you think it is within the power of a mother to destroy or elevate the image of the father?

A: When a mother has the greatest amount of time with a young person, they can forge or mold those young people into whatever they want them to be. They can fill them full of dogma. They can fill them full of fear. They can fill them full of positive aspect." [37]

So much of fatherhood depends on motherhood, for the good, virtuous, gentle daughter will become a good wife and mother; a bad, whiny, self-centered, lazy daughter — a bad wife.

Sirach 22:4–5

"A thoughtful daughter becomes a treasure to her husband, a shameless one is her father's grief. A hussy shames her father and her husband, by both she is despised."

Some may take comfort that their daughter is at least not a hussy, but what happened to modesty? Go out and see how your daughters dress and the ways they act. Maybe by today's "normal" behavior, they may not be viewed as immodest. But by the high, biblical standards of only a few decades ago, few from that era could describe today's dress and teenage girl behavior as "normal" or "feminine," — and they are to become mothers! How will we raise good fathers with lax and unvirtuous girls who are to become mothers? Little girls need to be raised not with the second rate aspirations of having a career, but to be a "mother," a queen of a little civilization that she will be entrusted with, where she will bring peace, soften harshness, and generate and foster a kingdom of love.

The following sad statement tears at the heart. What makes a grown man so indifferent, so hard, except the void somewhere of not having a mother to cancel the harshness of a father. Charles Francis Adams, a 19th century political fig ure and diplomat, recorded this entry in his diary:

> *"Went fishing with my son today — a day wasted."*

On the same day, his son, Brook Adams, wrote in his diary:

> *"Went fishing with my father today — the most wonderful day of my life."* [38]

The tragedy to a son's heart upon finding out that his father's thoughts were such would be devastating and likely the son would, by this indifference, become the same and perpetuate it to his sons.

How can it not be that the devastation to a son who is passed these bad traits by the bad example of a father be cancelled except by the interception of motherhood? **Yes, fatherhood is extremely important, but it comes through motherhood, and when there is a bad cycle, it must be broken and cancelled by a mother. It is precisely because of this that God the Father now sends "the Mother" to the world, the Virgin Mary, Mother of mothers.** Then what of men who have lifted up wayward boys who had no mother? Chances are you will find the one lifting them up had a good mother and if he didn't, he who lifted him up had the good mother. Motherhood is that powerful — to be able to pass through generations of people, affecting them through their sweet, good, and gentle nature.

June 6, 1989

> **"Dear children, 'the' Mother is happy to be with all of you...I want to speak to you about love and give you love..."**

It is up to the wives and mothers of the world to follow Our Lady's example — to reign and give love.

Bishop Fulton Sheen stated:

> *"The man governs the home but the woman*
> *reigns. Government is related to justice; reigning*
> *is related to love... The man is normally more se-*
> *rene than the woman, more absorbent of the dai-*
> *ly shocks of life, less disturbed by trifles. But on*
> *the other hand, in the great crises of life, it is the*
> *woman who, because of the gentle power of*
> *reigning, can give great consolation to man in his*
> *troubles. When he is remorseful, sad, and dis*
> *quieted, she brings comfort and assurance. As*
> *the surface of the ocean is agitated and troubled,*
> *but the great depths are calm, so in the really*
> *great catastrophes that affect the soul, the woman*
> *is the depth and the man the surface."*

Indeed, if the calm water below becomes agitated, on
the surface will be a very violent storm. One husband states:

> *"I know by the time I leave home in the morning*
> *if I will return to peace or to a war zone by my*
> *wife's attitude."*

The respect for authority the mother teaches the children comes back to her even when the father is away traveling,
or dies. James Dobson says that many times his father was

away, but that his father's impact on him was what made him
who he is today. Yet a large part of the image came from
James Dobson's mother. H.B. London, who is the cousin of
James Dobson and spent a lot of time with him growing up,
was asked about James Dobson's mother and her influence on
him as a child (James).

> H.B.: *"I think his mother's influence was crucial in
> that she loved him and showed her love for him
> even as she loved her husband and <u>showed</u> her love
> for her husband. But she always <u>elevated the rela-
> tionship with the husband.</u> Uncle Jimmy was the
> man of the house. He had just assumed the role of
> leader in the home and she responded to that leader-
> ship. She did not undermine his discipline while he
> was away from home. She maintained the same
> type of discipline and atmosphere in the home as
> though he was present.* [39]

Fatherhood can't prevail if the wife and mother does
not make every move to help it, to create it and mold her
children's image of it. Because of this, the wife can either
birth or abort it. Dr. James Egan, a child psychiatrist in
Washington, provocatively asserted:

> *"A dead father is a more effective father than a
> missing father. This is simply because when a fa-*

ther dies, he still maintains a place of authority, influence, and moral leadership in the house. Parents who have departed due to death usually leave a positive reputation. Their picture remains on the wall. They are talked about positively, and negative behavior on the part of a child can be corrected with a simple reminder, 'Would your dad have approved of that kind of behavior?'"

If this is the case, can it not also be said that positive or negative statements by the mother while the husband is at work will build a good or bad image of the father, regardless of whether he is perfect or not (because no father is)? What if he travels because of his job and is often away from home? What is the image the mother is building while he is gone? What of her statements, positive or negative, about the father made in the presence of the father when the children are also present?

A mother's power is immense. She has the ability by her actions and words toward the father to influence what kind of view the children will have of him. Today, few in society have a good, positive view of God the Father, and it is reflective of society's present view of earthly fathers. Many men, who leave their families, are today now coming forward and are relating that their wives drove them away. Surprisingly, many of them stated they wanted to be fathers, but their wives would not permit it. One relates:

> *"There is no question my wife wanted me to be a*
> *father and husband but dictated to me what kind of*
> *father I was supposed to be. Every initiative I*
> *made was vetoed, only to get up and try again. Fi-*
> *nally, though I still loved her, I could no longer*
> *stand her constant killing of my direction and I left.*
> *She wanted a family where everyone could do*
> *whatever they wanted. She got what she wanted*
> *because eventually there was no family left. I can*
> *honestly say she never allowed me to be the hus-*
> *band and father I felt I was supposed to be."*[40]

A mother undermines her future ability to govern if she lets her children do things while the father is not around, things that are not permitted by the father while he is home. Also, a mother who places her children, through words and actions, equal or above the husband does great harm to him and her children. By doing so she is telling them a father's position is not any more important than their own. If a father is held in view by the children as an equal, there will be little respect toward him or his desires. The children will grow in the view that their opinions carry just as much weight as the father's and eventually will break down as to why they can't do something when the father is of a different view. Today, in society, fathers are continually blamed and faulted as the culprit in so many family problems. However, many fathers are increasingly frustrated at their efforts to lead the family to a better tomorrow only to be shot down by the wife. One father relates:

> *"My son was arguing with me about a point in which he said I had no right to take action on. This challenge of his was not one in which I would back down on because the nature of his talking was abusive and an attack on my authority as a father. My wife entered and immediately said for the both of us to stop arguing, at which point my son became far more aggressive. He gained confidence and strength from his mother by these words of hers because she placed me as his equal, as two brothers arguing. Her words, rather than stopping the confrontation, inflamed matters further and I had to become more aggressive. The whole matter deteriorated. On the other hand, if she would have entered and said firmly, 'Son, how dare you show this kind of disrespect for your father? Stop arguing with your father,' it would have been a stabilizing effect, dissipating and debasing my son's challenge of my actions and my fatherhood. It would have brought back the recovery of peace much sooner."*[41]

A wife, placing her husband in this position, debases him and destroys his authority. But she will find herself and her position in exactly the same spot in the future. Her children will challenge her and treat her as their equal or place themselves above her. They learn this from the mother's behavior herself. She originates it, and her suffering will be far greater than that of the father. However, if she exalts the position of the husband, she will have a solid, respected future. As stated previously in these writings, a father is to be in the first place in affection and in love from his children.

One grown man relates a story about his mom, of how determined he was to follow out a decision and how he was twenty years old, at that! Yet his respect for her and her words had deep meaning and the assurance of being carried out because she herself had the same respect for his father while he was alive. He writes:

> *"Working my way through college was a hassle in itself but trying to find a place to park every-day only compounded the problems. Since my father had passed away only two years prior to my junior year of college, that also made things rough for Mom and I.*
>
> *"The solution came when one day I browsed through the showroom of a foreign motorscooter*

dealership. This was the solution to all sorts of problems: economical, affordable, never a problem to park, and I could save for a better car for after graduation. I carefully reviewed and answered every argument and objection I knew my mother would have. Just looking at facts and figures would be convincing in itself. Even though I knew she wanted nothing to do with her son on a motorcycle, she could not possibly deny that the whole idea made perfect sense. Besides, this was a motorscooter, not a motorcycle. Also, I was a mature twenty year old college student.

"One evening, after dinner, as I helped Mom with the dishes, I announced my plans on how I was going to be free of any more hassles with parking, being stuck in traffic, stopping for gas every other day, etc. When I finished, Mom never looked up but only said, 'Oh? I wonder where you are going to live?' The motorscooter remained in the showroom."

"My husband has decided he wants a divorce after 24 years of marriage. We are both Catholic, and I am a convert of 15 years. My faith is strong, his is faltering (for the last 3 years). He has been experiencing confusion and doubts about what he wants in life. He believes he has failed as husband and father, finances, etc. He wants to quit and get on with his life. His job is stressful for him, and he has a hard time handling anything else.

"We have been separated for two months. He is having a few second thoughts, and says he still loves me, but he doesn't know if he can live with us.

"I have been praying for the last four months or so for God's will to be done in his life. I don't believe in divorce and know what God's will is for married couples in the Bible. I also know we have our own free will. I trust that God is answering my prayer, and regardless of what happens, He will take care of me."

A letter from
Jacksonville, Florida

CHAPTER TWENTY

ARE WOMEN MORE IMPORTANT FOR THE STABILITY OF MEN, OR ARE MEN MORE IMPORTANT FOR THE STABILITY OF WOMEN?

After reading these writings, it might be said that so much emphasis is being put on the woman's submission and her role, still the question lingers — what about men? James Dobson, whom we already wrote of, is an internationally known advocate for the family with a ministry of 1200 employees assisting the restoration of the family. He states:

"Wives must understand and meet the unique needs of their husbands. That is an idea you may not have heard in a while. Let me be more specific. It is my conviction that Christian writers, myself included, have tended to overstate the masculine responsibilities in marriage and to understate the feminine. Men have been criticized for their failures at home, and yes, many of us deserve those criticisms. But women are imperfect people, too, and their shortcomings should

also be addressed. One of them is the failure of some wives to show respect and admiration for their husbands.

*"George Gilder, the brilliant social commentator and author of 'Men and Marriage,' believes **wo-men are actually more important to the stabili-ty and productivity of men than men are to the well-being of women**. I'm inclined to agree. When a wife believes in her husband and deeply respects him, he gains the confidence necessary to compete successfully and live responsibly. She gives him a reason to harness his masculine energy — to build a home, obtain and keep a job, remain sober, live within the law, spend money wisely, etc. Without positive feminine in-fluence, he may redirect the power of testosterone (a male hormone that is produced by the testes and is responsible for inducing and maintaining male secondary sex characters) in a way that is destructive to himself and to society at large."* [42]

So, a wife affects the ability of a husband to be her provider, her protector. If she is successful and lives for him, she benefits. If she fails and lives for her interests, she will live a desolate life with many sorrows. The book **Pathway of Life** states:

"Is man the child of sorrow, and do afflictions
and distresses pour their bitterness into his cup
(speaking of the husband)? How are his trials
alleviated, his sighs suppressed, his corroding
thoughts dissipated, his anxieties and pains re-
lieved, his gloom and depression chased away by
her (the wife's) cheerfulness and love? Is he
overwhelmed by disappointment, and mortified
by reproaches? There is one who can hide her
eyes even from his faults, and who, like her Fa-
ther who is in Heaven, can forgive and love
'without upbraiding.' And when he is sickened
by the subtleties and deception of the world;
when the acrimony of men has made him acri-
monious; when he becomes dissatisfied with him-
self, and all around him, her pleas and smile, her
undissembled tenderness, her artless simplicity,
restore him to himself, and spread serenity and
sweetness over his mind." [43]

While God the Father wants to give us everything, is it not we
who decide it by our love or indifference toward Him? The
more we obey and love Him the more He is able to gift us
with answering our prayers. And when we are indifferent to
God do we still expect Him to hear us? We determine a great
deal of our lives by how we live, just as the wife determines a

great deal of her own security by the way she relates to her husband.

> *"The good wife! How much of this world's hap-
> piness and prosperity is contained in the compass
> of these three short words! Her influence is im-
> mense. The power of a wife, for good or for evil,
> is altogether irresistible. Home must be the seat
> of happiness, or it must be forever unknown. A
> good wife is to a man wisdom, courage, strength,
> hope, and endurance. A bad one is confusion,
> weakness, discomfort, despair. No condition is
> hopeless when the wife possesses firmness, deci-
> sion, energy, economy. There is no outward
> prosperity which can counteract indolence, folly,
> and extravagance at home (of a bad wife). No
> spirit can long resist bad domestic influences.
> Man is strong, but his heart is not adamant. He
> delights in enterprise and action, but to sustain
> him he needs a tranquil mind and a whole heart.
> He expends his whole moral force in the conflicts
> of the world (at his daily jobs). His feelings are
> daily lacerated to the utmost point of endurance
> by perpetual collision, irritation, and disap-
> pointment (in his daily role of providing for his
> wife and family).*

"Let woman know, then, that she ministers at the very fountain of life and happiness. It is her hand that ladles out with overflowing cup its soul-refreshing waters, or casts in the branch of bitterness which makes them poison and death. Her ardent spirit breathes the breath of life into all enterprise. Her patience and constancy are mainly instrumental in carrying forward to completion the best human designs. Her more delicate moral sensibility is the unseen power which is ever at work to purify and refine society. And the nearest glimpse of heaven that mortals ever get on earth is that domestic circle which her hands have trained to intelligence, virtue, and love, which her gentle influence pervades, and of which her radiant presence is the center and the sun." [44]

Many would agree there are few who would be considered "gentlemen" in our society today. Why is that? How many women today are really sweet and gentle on a continued basis? Who is it but mothers that can teach gentleness to little boys and girls? Look at how few mothers today are truly gentle, and if it is so in public, does a gentle spirit truly prevail to their children behind closed doors? Until we have real and true "gentle-wives," "gentle-mothers," we will never have "gentlemen."

Once we again have "gentlemen," we can expect better treatment of wives, that will result in better marriages and healing of society and the world. **Pathway of Life** states:

> *"A good marriage is the healing of the world.*
> *Marriage is the mother of the world, and pre-*
> *serves kingdoms and fills cities and churches and*
> *heaven itself."* [45]

Because marriage is the "mother" of the world of life, satan, lucifer, the angel of darkness disguised as light, with all his millions of deformed demon angels, wants the "center," the working structure of marriages; that is, submission and obedience destroyed. In this way he has during our time gained eternal power over multitudes, and will continue to do so.

So, must we still ask ourselves why is the center falling apart? Why are so many homes fatherless, husbands leaving — totally abandoning their homes? If it were a haven for him, it would make little logic for him to leave. And what was the advice of the good wife when she stood by her husband in great difficulty and when her daughter planned to take action against her husband in the bed? How many wives have pushed their husbands out the door into someone else's arms? Yet Our Lady is showing us to rectify and reconcile. Peace must be brought into the house, husbands won back, and relationships built. In the **Poem of the Man-God**, Jesus speaks of the husbands who are driven away by various trifles of the wives:

> *"Is the husband honest? A stupid jealousy, by driving him out of the house, exposes him to the danger of falling into the snares of a prostitute. Is he not honest and faithful? The fury of a jealous wife will not correct him, but her grave attitude, free from grudge and rudeness, her dignified and loving, still loving behavior, will make him ponder and return to reason. <u>Learn how to win back your husbands</u>, when a passion separates them from you, through your virtue, just as you conquered them in your youth through your beauty. And, to gain strength for such duty, and resist the grief which might make you unfair, love your children and consider their welfare."* [46]

Yes, children need a father. But fatherhood has been crippled by the rebellion of women against motherhood in varying degrees. Both parents are needed. In the book **Jesus Called Her Mother**, the author Dee Jepsen writes:

> *"Children need two healthy adult role models and energy is sapped by fruitless jockeying for power and position. Just the opposite spirit ap-*

pears to prevail in the marriage of Mary and Joseph." [47]

Jockeying for power between two individuals in a marriage will always be the case when God's ordained order is not adhered to. From these two individuals in a child's life will be taught all the formation of living and working in society. If they see just authority from the father, the gracious receiving of that authority from the wife, the dignity of God the Father in their father, the awe and respect of the wife towards her husband, then the children will be whole; all they can be. And if the children fall, it will not be because of the parents. But rather than stay fallen, the parents, having given their children this formation, give them the ability to get up and get straight.

Proverbs 22:6

"Train up a child in the way he should go, and when he is old he will not depart from it."

Too many parents do not understand the core of the problem with children, and they give bad advice not only by word but by their actions, especially in relations between each other.

Our Lady said on October 24, 1988:

> **"Dear children, your Mother wants to call you to pray for the young of the whole world, for the parents of the whole world so they know how to educate their children and how to lead them in life with good advice. Pray, dear children; the situation of the young is difficult. Help them! Help parents who don't know, who give bad advice."**

Children learn from their parents. A rebellious wife will produce rebellious children no matter what the husband counters it with. Maria Valtorta writes of Jesus' words in the **Poem of the Man-God**:

> *"Their innocent eyes (children) look at you, they study you and they understand more than you think, and they 'mould' their spirits according to what they see and understand. Never scandalize your innocent children."* [48]

In Medjugorje, Our Lady told Jelena, the innerlocutionist, that children learn even how to love by watching their two parents love and respect each other. In an interview by Jan Connell from the book, **The Visions of the Children**, Jelena states:

Q: Tell me more about young people and their parents.

A: The Blessed Mother says God intended love and respect between parents and children. Then the relationship will be happy.

Q: How do parents and children achieve this love and respect?

A: By watching and emulating the love and respect <u>between</u> the mother and father.

Q: But if there is no love and respect between the husband and wife, this can poison future generations.

A: Without prayer, fasting, and sacrificial love by both mother and father, family harmony is impossible." [49]

So where we began was the "how to" in the proper raising of children, and the first and primary foundation is a strong center. Through this the children will grow and flourish in an ordered home which allows love to flow in through God's blessing. Once you receive God's blessing, how is it maintained? According to Maria Valtorta's writings, Jesus says:

> "And reverting to how the members of a family
> and the inhabitants of a house should be, so that
> My blessing may remain, be respectful and ob-
> edient, so that you may be so also with the Lord
> your God. Because if you do not learn to obey
> the simple orders of your fathers and mothers,
> whom you see, how will you be able to obey the
> commands of God, which are given to you in His
> name, but you neither see nor hear Him? And if
> you do not learn to believe that he who loves, as
> a father and a mother love, can but order good
> things, how can you believe that the things, which
> are related to you as commands of God, are
> good? God loves, you know, and is a Father.
> And just because He loves you and wants you to
> be with Him, dear children, He wants you to be
> good. And the first school where you learn to
> become so is your family. You learn there to
> love and to obey and there begins for you the
> way that leads to Heaven. So be good, respect-
> ful, docile. Love your fathers also when they
> correct you, because they do so for your own
> good, and love your mothers if they restrain you

from doing actions which by their experience
they know are not good." [50]

So clearly children learn to obey by the father's submission to God the Father, and the mother's submission to the husband. But still, what of those who, as the girls smirking on the retreat, do not accept this — that as Scripture states a husband will be their lord? Take note of a warning from a statement by a father of five sons:

"I am raising and teaching my sons to steer clear
of any girl who is rebellious, fusses a lot, or
whines. That rebellion will turn into war. Fuss-
ing will turn into the killing of any joy you wake
up with and whining will turn into nagging once
you have married these types of girls." [51]

He noted that within a week his 18-year-old broke up with a girl he had been dating for months. When asked why by the father, he replied, *"She fusses too much!"*

Still some mothers may respond that boys just won't find anybody then, for my girls are going to go to college, have a career, will be independent and won't be bossed! Beware and remember the young boys on retreat shaking their heads in agreement about men are to be the heads of the family. God is dealing deep within the spirit of manhood in the present time. **Fatherhood is coming and in the next few years all will see by God the Father's design, a rebirth of Father-hood. It is part of Our Lady's plans. It is welling up. Already football stadiums across the country are being filled with fifty thousand or more men, all gathering with the express purpose to take up their role as shepherds. In the next few years, on all fronts, "<u>fatherhood is the coming societal change.</u>"** If mothers don't begin teaching their little daughters how to be mothers instead of "finding a career" and "doing for self," then these little girls, once grown-up, are most likely going to end up being obsolete and old maids.

"This book helped me see how I was using a pick and choose effort in submission. This effort was still unfruitful as I was having my way while enduring much chaos in my home recently. After reading this book and through prayer, it was like a floodgate opening. I was able to see so clearly what was happening and I could almost literally feel burdens lift from me, and I can also feel a new-found hopefulness. I have six children and I was in desperate need from God on what to do with my marriage and my husband. It's a hard pill to swallow, but I know with repeated efforts it is bound to go down!"

A letter from
Morse, Louisiana

CHAPTER TWENTY-ONE

I'M CHRISTIAN. I DO WHAT MY HUSBAND WANTS...WELL MOST OF THE TIME...

Many women who read this may say, *"This is for the next woman. I'm an obedient wife."* A great deal of denial is taking place. Wives who say, *"I'm obedient **most** of the time,"* and who believe this is enough are highly destructive. Their actions of "sometimes" doing their own thing are dangerous to, not only their families, but society and future generations as well. Elizabeth Rice Handford states:

> *"The woman who submits to her husband will share a oneness with him, a communion she never dreamed of, an emotional peace and security positively **<u>unattainable</u>** when she struggles with him for power in the home."* [52]

Okay! So that's understood. But how can it be that damaging to my family and future generations by only occasionally not doing what my husband asks? One Christian wife and mother in a conversation at a dentist office commented, *"Oh yes, I believe I am supposed to obey my husband, and I do most of the time."* When asked what "most of the time" meant, she answered, *"I submit unless I feel there is something else I want to do."* A wife who follows her husband only when it is agreeable to her, even if she is obedient 90%, or even 99% of the time, cannot bring blessings and total peace to her home, nor live love to the fullest for her husband and family. If a wife "does her own thing," even if just occasionally, but goes against her husband's direction in doing so, though not apparent immediately, she will create unbelievable damage in her family. A pure glass of water is 100% pure until a drop of potent poison is placed in it. It then becomes a glass of poison. Even if a Christian woman is 99% obedient, the 1% disobedience will lead to the destruction of the woman's peace and it <u>will</u> damage her children, as well as her husband.

For those who may doubt the above, there are many examples of wives throughout history who have **"<u>mostly</u>"** obeyed their husbands, but on some "singular" occasion did not. The Bible shows many times that a single act of disobedience to the husband, bending or compromising his direction, can do incalculable damage even for thousands of years. Of course Eve is the first and most known example, but others follow in Scripture. Elizabeth Rice Handford writes of Scripture:

> *"When a woman usurps the spiritual leadership of the home, **<u>it always leads to tragedy</u>**. Sarah*

*thought she had a solution to what was basically
a spiritual problem — her barrenness. God had
already promised her a son, but she got impatient
and unbelieving. She suggested Abraham take
Hagar, her maid. The child of that union, Ishmael, brought estrangement and heartache, and
millenniums of conflict between Arab and
Jew."* [53]

A mother and wife should never discount the bad fruit
of usurpation and disobedience. It is not just a physical matter, but a matter of the heart as well. If Jesus says adultery
committed in the heart is a sin the same as the act being carried out is, then how can it be reconciled that a wife be obedient physically, yet in her heart is rebellion with a desire to
usurp or compromise her husband's direction? She who does
not physically commit adultery, but continues the sin in her
heart, **will** eventually commit it physically if given the opportunity. So rebellion in the heart will eventually manifest itself
physically, if not squelched. You've read already that there
has to exist an attitude in the heart to please and obey. Love
and a strong desire to obey **must** replace rebellious feelings of
the heart. This **will** bring happiness. Peace and happiness
cannot come, even if obedience and submission are being performed, if within the heart disrespect and rebelliousness are
harbored. Women will gain everything by nurturing in their
hearts an attitude to please and obey their husbands. They

will lose a great deal by not doing so. Another case from
Scripture involves Moses:

> *"Moses, saved from death by his mother's faith,*
> *rejecting the splendor of Pharaoh's court, mis-*
> *taking the way to redeem his people from their*
> *bondage, fled to the wilderness. During his forty*
> *years of exile, he married Zipporah, an Ethio-*
> *pian, daughter of the priest of Midian. Two sons*
> *were born to them.*
>
> *"Then Moses met God face to face. God com-*
> *missioned him to give Pharaoh a message:*
> *'Israel is my first-born. Let him go free.' Moses*
> *put his wife and sons on an ass and went back to*
> *Egypt to free his people. They stopped at an inn*
> *in Egypt for the night.*
>
> *"But what is this? A form wrestles with Moses*
> *and seeks to kill him. Who is it? The Lord!*
> *God Himself is trying to kill Moses! But why?*
> *Why would God try to kill the man he had just*
> *sent to redeem Israel? It is the child, Gershom.*
> *He is not circumcised! The sign of the covenant*
> *between Israel and God, commanded to be ex-*
> *ecuted upon every son — Moses has broken the*
> *covenant! But he cannot save himself — God*

holds him in the grip of death, and Moses is help-
less to correct his fault.

"Zipporah seizes a sharp stone, circumcises the
child, throws the foreskin down at Moses' feet.
God is satisfied. Moses is released.

"What does all this mean? How did Zipporah
know what was needed? Zipporah was not a
Jew, perhaps was not a believer. (Her father was
not, until he saw the wonders God did in bring-
ing Israel out of Egypt — Exod. 18:8–11). How
did she know why God was about to kill her
husband? The clue is found in what she said to
her husband: 'Thou art a bloody husband to me.'
Evidently Moses had intended to circumcise the
child, and Zipporah had protested that it was
'too bloody.' She evidently did not like the aes-
thetics of her husband's bloody religion. How-
ever, to save her husband's life, she would cir-
cumcise the child, but still in rebellion.

"They did not continue the journey together.
Aaron found Moses back at the Mount of God
and went with him back to Egypt to accomplish
his great task. Zipporah stayed in Midian with

her father until after the children of Israel came out of Egypt.

"By interfering with her husband's spiritual leadership in the home, she nearly caused his death. She lost all the reward of being a helpmate to her husband (and how he must have needed it in those overwhelming days!) in the greatest crisis of his life. And, judging from the importance given it throughout Scripture, she missed being a part of one of the most glorious events in the history of mankind." [54]

Elizabeth Rice Handford offers more examples from the Bible of the great harm done which comes from ignoring God's order and structure, even if only on occasion or when just slightly bending it.

"Genesis 27 tells the story of Rebekah's conspiracy against her aged, blind husband Isaac. She wanted her favorite, the younger son Jacob, to receive his patriarchal blessing. (How many lessons we could learn from that sad family relationship, when father and mother chose favorites and fostered jealousy between the children!) She went to great lengths to deceive him, and the woe that followed her deception can hardly be up:

*Esau's murderous hatred, Jacob's banishment
for twenty-one toil-filled years. And all of it, **all**
of it, was unnecessary because God Himself had
promised Rebekah, before the twins were born,
that 'the elder shall serve the younger' (Gen.
25:23). When that poor wife started managing
(and muddling) the spiritual affairs of her home,
she snarled all the good things God intended to
accomplish in His own good time.*

*"Consider the terrible results when the wife of a
king sets out to manage the spiritual life of the
home. King Solomon was 'beloved by God,'
wonderfully endowed. He was the child of King
David, who God had promised would always
have a son to sit on the throne of David. But Solomon's wives 'turned away his heart after other
gods.' The supremely blessed Solomon, wiser
than any other man, builder of the Temple of the
most high God, stooped to building temples for
the wicked idols of his wives (I Kings 11:1–13).
The division of the kingdom and a thousand
years of civil war were the terrible price paid because one man let his wives assume the spiritual
leadership of the home."* [55]

Biblical, as well as secular history, shows God is not lax in His dealings with a wife who usurps and with a husband who follows. When women or men allow a reversal of God's order, as the Bible truths show, **disaster will follow**. It is a guarantee. The smallest of violations, if continued, may add up to a family's suicide. Today's society clearly suffers from this challenge to male authority.

Today it is said that women are discriminated against, put down, abandoned, many times treated as second class citizens, and on and on. The fact is, it is true!! Society is correct in saying that women today are treated as second-class, that they are degraded, are not valued, etc... However, society is dead wrong as to the reasons and the solutions. How can a material thing or any person be of value when it or they do not do that which they were made to do? What good is a car that won't run? What kind of value would children place on a mother who is home everyday when they return from school as opposed to the value children would have of a mother who is not home for several hours after they return from school? Ask the children in these situations; ask the husband. Will a husband value a wife more who makes a home as opposed to a wife who does not? What of a wife who is rebellious compared to one who is not? What of a wife who is of a sweet disposition versus one who is not? It should not be a wonder why women have lost a great deal of respect and admiration. It is true women are in need of emancipation, but the emanci-

pation from the bondage from which women suffer and a
need to be freed is not subjection. Rather, women need to be
freed from freedom, the "freedom to do as one pleases,"
which is what the meaning of emancipation is. Webster Dictionary defines the word this way:

> **Emancipate** — to release from "<u>paternal care</u>"
> and "<u>responsibility</u>;" to <u>free from</u> "<u>restraint</u>,"
> "<u>control</u>," or the "<u>power of another</u>." [56]

The Christian life is "**<u>responsibility</u>**." Every Christian is to
care for a brother with "**<u>paternal care</u>**." To follow Christ is to
live under constant "**<u>restraint</u>**," to be under **"<u>control</u></u>."** The
Church is built upon authority of a certain "**<u>power over ano-
ther</u>**," not for negative results but for positive results. In the
Church, priests are under the authority of their bishops; the
bishops, under the authority of the pope. In secular society,
the vice president is under the authority of the president, the
assistant coach is under the head coach. Yet society says
women are to be free of any and all restraints? This is the
<u>cause</u> of the bondage from which they now suffer. Freedom
will be found in their obedience to their roles as laid out in
Scripture. Yes, women are degraded in today's society. **And
yet, it is the forsaking of wifehood and motherhood to self-
interest and self-fulfillment that has led to the present intoler-
able conditions.** The bad fruit which has come from following
self has led to the continuation and furthering of the yelling

voice of society enraged over women's suffrage and rights. And yet, women's pursuit of these things has actually "dethroned" them, therefore causing more suffering and the loss of more rights. The voice of society escalates and becomes louder in regard to the wrongs committed against women, many of which are legitimate, but stem from reasons that are illegitimate, namely the birthing of authority out of "wedlock." **To claim authority by bypassing male authority is outside the God-ordained structure, just as a child conceived out of wedlock would be illegitimate as opposed to a child conceived in wedlock. In other words, women can have authority, just as women can get pregnant. This authority must be legitimate within God's structure, just as getting pregnant must be within the confines of marriage to be considered legitimate. Therefore, it is illegitimate to claim a "right" of equal authority with man as God-ordained. This is not true, equal authority does not exist even if man invents it.**

Our Lady is coming to raise the dignity of women by helping place them in respected positions. Our Lady is doing this through Her example as a mother as well as through signs to us to show that She, too, is under authority and has a position to fill. Through Our Lady accepting the position of "servant" with a perfect attitude of servitude and lowliness, Her dignity has been raised beyond measure.

Marija reveals a startling and remarkable fact about Our Lady's appearances. A famous theologian was speaking to her about the way Our Lady dresses when She comes. Marija told him Our Lady comes in a grey dress, simple, beautiful, because the color is from heaven, yet, a basic grey dress. The theologian explained to Marija that the color grey is considered the color of servitude and that Our Lady's coming in this color is significant. She wants to identify Herself as a servant because Our Lady is coming to serve. The color gray would be a typical "color" worn by a servant. Our Lady makes a tremendous statement by appearing this way. She is serving as a servant mother.

When women understand the magnitude of who Our Lady is, "The" Queen of all Heaven and Earth, who at the same time, **<u>chooses</u>** servitude, they should want to vie for this position. By imitating this beautiful example as lived by Our Lady, the esteem, respect, dignity and love shown towards women will steadily increase among society. These are all things women have suffered the loss of, and because of this loss, they go more and more in the wrong direction trying to achieve them. The following quote is from Pope John Paul II:

> *"The Church sees in Mary the highest expression of the 'feminine genius,' and she finds in her a source of constant inspiration. Mary called herself the 'handmaid of the Lord' (Lk 1:38).*

Through obedience to the Word of God she ac-cepted her lofty yet not easy vocation as wife and mother in the family of Nazareth. Putting herself at God's service, she also put herself at the ser-vice of others: a service of love. Precisely through this service Mary was able to experience in her life a mysterious, but authentic 'reign.' It is not by chance that she is invoked as 'Queen of Heaven and earth.' The entire community of be-lievers thus invokes her; many nations and peoples call upon her as their 'Queen.' For her, 'to reign' is to serve! Her service is 'to reign!'" [57]

"I have a friend who for years has sown nothing but rebellion in her family, while all the time thinking she was doing good and being a good mom. She is a nice person, but her rebellion against her husband and her ridiculing him has led to much dissension and with that destruction within the family. All the while she has become more and more dissatisfied with her family. I am at a loss of what to do to make her see that what she blames on her husband is mostly of her own doings."

> *A letter from*
> *Fargo, North Dakota*

CHAPTER TWENTY-TWO

A WIFE DESTROYED

What of those wives who today are either disenchanted or see the grass is greener on the other side of the fence? It is a fact, a guarantee, a given, that without a doubt those who go to the next pasture will suffer misery one-hundred-fold compared to their present situations. Wrongs or sins can never lead to a "bettering" of your life. For a while it may seem so, but women who set out on this path will suffer loss of identity, purpose, self worth, and their mission of wifehood and motherhood. The columnist Ann Landers published the following letter:

August 18, 1995

"Dear Ann Landers: I know you receive many 'learn-from-my-mistake' letters, but I hope you will print just one more. My husband of two decades said he was tired of the utility bills, tired of our children being less than he expected, and too tired to talk or go anywhere or do much of anything with me and the kids. His job was more

217

*important than his family. He denied it, but his
actions spoke louder than his words.*

*"I met a man who said he liked my hair, my eyes
and my mind. Eventually, he told me he loved
me. My husband left me alone one night too
many, and I packed my bags and took off with
the man who liked my hair, my eyes and my
mind.*

*"It is now three years later. Maybe some women
who leave home and family actually find what
they are looking for. I didn't. I lost my identity,
my purpose, my sense of self-worth and my mission in life. A thousand times over, I've prayed
to God: <u>Please, I want to go home.</u>*

*"Remember this letter, you wives and mothers
who are feeling unappreciated and unloved. The
'solution' is not out there. Stay where you are,
and work it out."*

Life Destroyed

There is little doubt this woman killed her entire life
and that she sincerely believed her husband's faults sparked
it. However, with a little wisdom can we not see another side
of the picture? The husband was tired, too tired to talk or go

anywhere, tired of the bills. Is it possible that her wants kept him having to work? Did their standard of living prevent him from working less? Did she offer to move to a less expensive place to lower expenses in order that the husband would not have to work so much? She states his job was more important than family, yet she states he denied that. This is the give-away, and yet she refuses to believe that that may just be the case. Why would he be tired, exhausted, not even wanting to talk with her? What was it that made him this way, unless he was feeling pressure to provide and meet the wants of his wife, combined with not having a haven for a home? His denial that his work was more important than family was very possibly the truth. Evidently to **him** it was the truth, as this is the case with many husbands today.

She said that he told her the kids were less than he expected. Did she water down his expectations and standards? Did she follow through on his direction for his children? If she did, why was he disappointed? Many women would be surprised to discover that they have created problems which they do not see, blaming husbands for conditions which they themselves have made, placing pressure to "do," "go," "have," "be," all of which requires providing the resources for them and usually means a lot of work. Many wives today have husbands in a no-win situation. The foregoing letter reveals all of these things as well as the wife's blindness to the fact that she herself may have been a large part of the prob-

lem in the beginning, as well as in the end, with her adultery.
It's very possible that this family would be together today if
the wife had had the wisdom to see ways in the beginning to
follow her husband's direction. A good indication that she
wasn't doing this is her statement that the children were less
than what her husband expected. Her stating this shows a
conflict that what he expected out of the children, she did not.
Was it she who lowered these expectations against her husband's direction? This is a common problem in families today.

It is true that to be Christian, to walk with Christ, there
will be sufferings and crosses to accept along the way. But
with the demands God places upon us come also His promises. Scripture states in Jeremiah 29:11:

> *"'For I know well the plans I have in mind for
> you,' says the Lord, 'plans for your welfare, not
> for woe! Plans to give you a future full of
> hope.'"*

If we wake up one morning and find that we have lost **<u>every-
thing</u>** dear to us, "**<u>everything</u>**" that gave meaning to our
lives, then we must reflect on the decisions we were responsible for making that led to these events taking place. God
does not abandon his children. If the woman in the letter
chose the path of submission, she **<u>would</u>** have seen her situa-

tion turn around, her family healed, and joy and contentment in her own life again.

It's not to say the husband was without fault, or even perhaps he could have been stronger. But here again we have the same pattern that society follows of, *"Look what the husband caused."* Too many husbands are simply getting fed up and leaving. One wife, in seeking advice, explained her situation. Her husband, without warning, came home on her birthday and said he wanted a divorce and left. She was devastated, angry, and couldn't believe he did this on her birthday and with two kids. However, the advisor, suspicious that there was much more to the story because of the husband's purposely leaving on her birthday, sought more information from her. He found she nagged, put down, complained, had things her way, withheld bedroom privileges, and on and on. Her husband had tried and tried to make her see his agitation until finally he became convinced she would never change. His anger and frustration was such he wanted to pay her back with vengeance, hence, a birthday abandonment. He never returned, his love even killed for his children, and she readily admits now much of it was her fault. Though she is truly repentant and sorry, there is nothing she can do on a human level; only by prayer will there be an answer for her situation.

Every act of disobedience is presently coming under God's wrath in the present time. It is God who wants to puri-

fy the family of that which is destroying it, and families that
resist coming into good order will not stay in union together.
There now exists a clear cleansing of the family, and satan is
reaping the harvest with the power to kill the family through
the resistance of God's ordained order. satan is now released
upon the world to put through fire and trial all dissidents to
obedience. It is easy for all those who are in prayer and do
not want to be deceived to see what is happening.

> *"Let no one deceive you with empty arguments,*
> *for because of these things the wrath of God is*
> *coming upon the disobedient."* (Ephesians 5:6)

Indeed, it is as at the first passover. The blood over our door-
post is prayer. Families are coming under attack as the firstborn were thousands of years ago. We are protected when we
put the Blood of the Lamb, which is "prayer" and "obedience," in our home. All others who do not will experience
the deteriorating damage of the assassin of peace. Where
there is no peace, families eventually die.

August 25, 1995

> "Dear children! Today I invite you to prayer.
> Let prayer be life for you. A family cannot say
> that it is in peace if it does not pray. Therefore,
> let your morning begin with morning prayer,

**and the evening end with thanksgiving. Little
children, I am with you, and I love you and I
bless you and I wish for everyone of you to be in
my embrace. You cannot be in my embrace if
you are not ready to pray everyday. Thank you
for having responded to my call."**

This should not strike fear in the hearts of Our Lady's children. God promises every good thing to all those who obey
His commands. If we always strive to do our best, we should
stand with confidence before the Father who desires with in-
tensity to give us all that Heaven holds.

As these writings are being read by you, many mistakes we all have made may become clear to you. Many times
this is a source of grief and suffering, to realize mistakes that
were made and to know nothing can be done about it. If Jesus does not condemn the woman adulteress, then no one can
condemn anyone, no matter how grave the wrong may have
been. The hope we have is that Our Lady knows we have
been a rebellious people. She knows the terrible past mistakes we have made with our husbands and wives, and how
we have damaged our children. It is for this reason Our Lady
repeatedly, in the last several years, starts her messages with
the word, **"Today"**; **"Start to live from 'Today' my messages."**
We cannot rectify the past, but from this moment forward,
today, if we start, Our Lady will slowly, over time, heal our

mistakes as much as possible without violating our free will.
Our future is one of hope, even in the midst of many wrongs,
but <u>only</u> if we start living Her messages **"Today."**

  Many sacramental unions have been damaged or
killed. We noted Ivan says this happens when at least one
spouse commits a grave sin against the marriage, and then satan gains power in the family. <u>A good place to kill satan in</u>
<u>the family is to renew your family, to restore or resurrect the</u>
<u>sacramental union through the restating of the marriage vows.</u>
This will allow God to grant more graces and blessings upon
you to heal your family. It should not be rushed into but rather prepared for with novenas and much prayer. Once done,
you can expect to experience more strength in your relationship as well as in love. Ivan was asked why couples in the last
few decades have had so many troubles or struggles:

> A: *How did they enter into their marriage? Did*
> *they have any type of preparing for marriage?*
> *If they didn't then later it could cause many*
> *troubles in their marriage. You need to have*
> *some sort of balance. I mean you need to*
> *have a meaning for your life, your children's*
> *lives. You need to have faith in the heart of*
> *your family. There is one thing you need to*
> *understand — that all people need to know:*
> *Marriage is holy and it is supposed to mean*

something to us. Holy is not just a word, it has meaning. So if we follow the rules that the Church gave us and have faith in God, have faith in the Virgin Mary, __we are going to have a near perfect life__, with all the good and bad things because nobody except God is perfect." [58]

To start a new beginning and to heal the past of serious wrongs and rebellion, make plans to restate your marriage vows; to restore or resurrect your marriage or rather your Sacramental union. This is the place to start, but only through special preparation.

In Medjugorje remarkable events occur. Following these happenings, one can realize the desires of Our Lady.

Angela*, an Italian woman from Italy, had decided to make a pilgrimage to Medjugorje with a group. A second Italian group, with no knowledge of the first group, also planned a pilgrimage to Medjugorje. One of the travelers on the second group was Michael*, an Italian who had divorced 20 years before. Both groups were in Medjugorje at the same time.

As God masterfully ordains everything, the two groups happened to make the climb up Cross Mountain on the same day. As each group climbed, they prayed the fourteen stations, climbing their Calvary. As those who have climbed know, many wrongs of your past flash up, and a grace of true repentance comes to many hearts. The mountain is a place of spiritual miracles. Upon arriving on the mountain, groups kneel and pray at the foot of the giant cross. The two Italian groups came face to face. It was there, at the foot of the cross, that Michael and Angela came face to face. They were stunned and shocked. The two knew each other and <u>had not seen</u> each other for twenty years! You see, Angela was also divorced twenty years before to the man who now stood beside her before the cross. They talked and prayed together. News spread throughout the whole village of Medjugorje, and when the divorced couple decided to take up their married life again, the village overflowed with a contagious JOY!! Everyone was in praise and marveled at Our Lady's intercession to bring the divorced couple back together.

This story shows Our Lady's desire to CANCEL divorces and restore the Sacramental Union.

---

* The names have been changed.

CHAPTER TWENTY-THREE

I WANT TO REPAIR MY SACRAMENTAL UNION!

A priest from Australia wrote of a couple who prepared for marriage in an incredible way. This story serves as
an example of how renewing your marriage vows or saying
them for the first time should be:

Dear Caritas,   *June 7, 1995*

*"May the God of our Lord Jesus Christ enlighten
your innermost <u>vision</u> that you may know the great
hope to which He has called you, the wealth of his
glorious heritage to be distributed among the members of the church, and the immeasurable scope of
His power in us who believe. That vision of faith is
much more important. I should like to thank you
for all the newsletters, the monthly world-given messages from Medjugorje, and the novena booklets.
On the novena booklets, I would like to share an
experience with you. I celebrated the marriage of
two young people who are deeply committed to the*

Lord and to the Blessed Virgin Mother. During the months of pre-marriage counseling and preparation we — the couple, the bridal party, and myself prayed five novenas, at least two of which,* and maybe three of them were from your booklet. The last one on the ninth night we finished during a time of adoration of the Blessed Sacrament. The ten members of the bridal party, myself, the two adult servers at the Mass, plus some of the members of the music ministry, spent nearly two hours around the altar on which the Blessed Sacrament was exposed. We also read and reflected on and shared our thoughts on the Scripture readings the couple had chosen for their wedding ceremony and the blue-print of their life together. It was a rich and enrich-ing faith experience for all of us. In addition, <u>the bride and bride-groom carried out a fast for 40 days before their wedding.</u> Just as Jesus fasted for forty days before He began his mission, so Justin and Sandra saw their marriage ceremony as the com-

---

* These seven novenas (one said each month beginning on the 25th of each month) are the novenas which you have already read about and are being prayed as a result of the apparition on Thanksgiving Day (November 24, 1988) in the Field to heal our nation, all of which was birthed from over the marriage bed of the couple who submitted to God's plans. A simple "yes" to God speaks of the great power of submission in that, from this bed to the opposite side of the world in Australia, many are being affected by what was birthed from over this bed and perhaps millions will be affected in the future.

mencement of their mission to be a faithful husband and wife, to be a good father and a good mother.

"With such a spiritual preparation one expected the wedding ceremony to be blessed — and it was blessed abundantly. People said they felt something special when they came into the church. The Spirit's presence was very obvious and many hearts were touched, some were very profoundly touched.

"I based my homily on the marriage preparation we undertook, to touch the hearts of young people preparing for marriage. After the wedding reception banquet, the newly marrieds returned to the church to say the Rosary in the presence of the Blessed Sacrament as we have adoration of the Blessed Sacrament all day Friday and through Friday night and Saturday until the commencement of the vigil Mass at 6:30 p.m. I thought you might appreciate that your prayerful novenas could be put to good use in far away Australia (down under). We praise God."

Yours sincerely in Jesus and Mary,
City Beach, West Australia / a Priest

There are probably very few marriages which would not benefit by the restating of the vows, and if a couple prepared as the couple did in the letter, how greatly would their lives and families improve!! Begin praying, head toward the repairing of any damage to your sacramental union or toward the resurrection of one which is dead. It will be a new beginning for you. Many now who are married admit they didn't even realize what they were saying when they married. Our Lady wants reconciliation. She wants restoration. The grace and joy will be great, but you must begin those steps "today."

The bed Our Lady appeared over, its meaning, and purposes of marriage and family influenced the foregoing letter from Australia. For those who will renew their marriage vows, the example the priest wrote about of the couple marrying is a beautiful one to imitate. How could a bed, located at a certain spot on the earth, represent marriage, family, and society and have such a far-reaching impact as to affect families on the other side of the earth, unless everything has a center? As scientists thought the atom was the final center and later discovered revolutions taking place within it, that it was a little universe; so too the sacramental union is yet another center. While the wife revolves around the husband, they both revolve around their sacramental union, their oneness, the point from which they receive grace from God for their marriage. The sacramental union should be prayed for and maintained by both in prayer, while begging God's grace upon it, to strengthen it, to shower His love upon it, and to drape it in His mercy if it is hurt, or has been injured. Pray for its resurrection if it's been murdered by rebellion and sin. The serious restating of the marriage vows will re-create the sacramental union just as a blackened soul which is dead from mortal sin, and which is revived by serious confession to become the purest of white, splendid in the eyes of God, shining before the angels.

Mid June, 1985

"...man's heart is like this splendid pearl. When he belongs completely to the Lord, he shines even in the darkness. But when he is divided, a little to satan, a little to sin, a little to everything, he fades and is no longer worth anything."

Bringing the sacramental union to full life, to a hunger for life, will be achieved by your preparing, fasting, and praying for it, then by renewing your vows. Pure and holy love will be enkindled between you through the restating and resurrection of your vows — sacramental union. If prepared for as the Australian couple did, glorious will this sacramental union be as it appears before God. Years of damage and its fruits will not be remedied overnight, but rather than bad fruit, new fruit, good fruit will begin to be harvested, increasing yearly as more prayer and blessings are poured forth on your sacramental union.

We must realize this sacramental union exists; it is not thin air. Are we to deny it is real, has life, as abortionists deny that the womb contains life? So many of us have aborted this sacramental union. We have damaged it with our anger, and then left it injured without trying to cure it, without trying to heal it by going to our spouse to reconcile. Instead, we come in and cut it with our silence or violent words, again adding injury on top of injury. How it lies there bleeding, being ripped to pieces by strife, as an infant is ripped to pieces, torn from the womb. How dare we condemn abortionists when we ourselves are doing the same thing to the sacramental union. Is this statement too much? Too strong? Is the comparison out of balance? Hardly, when what we are doing is killing society when we kill our children's spirit through the killing of our spouse's spirit. This gives satan control over the entire family by our formal invitation. This kind of killing might originate as an argument, unjust act, selfishness, etc. It is where real abortions start. The sacramental union is the center. When you damage or destroy it, disorder occurs in the outer limits of society. Does not a damaged or killed sacramental union result in separation, divorce, or a broken home? Do not statistics easily prove that broken homes have resulted in an explosion of teenage pregnancies? Do not most of these teens get abortions? Just because one does not divorce is no excuse. Actions which injure your sacramental union contribute to abortions. The aborted babies' blood is on our hands. We are not without guilt, even if our homes do not break up. When we cause a chill in our home colder than Antarctica, do we not weaken the spirit of our children which, in turn, weakens society, which has brought about the great sins such as abortion? Where has our wisdom gone? We don't pray, so we no longer have the ability to see the indirect fruit of our own sins! We no longer have the wisdom to trace the repercussions of our actions and to see where it has all led. Many of us are going to be very surprised at our judgement, at how much we have contributed to many things to which we are opposed. Our Lady now comes to give us this wisdom. The evidence and guilt are there, and anyone who loves truth and desires it will learn what we must do to clean up our act. It will be through obedience and submission to God and His ways. Once you grasp the problem, go to it's center and then, <u>only</u> then, will you become truly one. The wife submits in everything to her husband and the husband to God the Father. It will be a blending of the two wills into one. **"Wo Man"** is one but if you are married and remain **man** and **woman "2"**, you will have to do what so many counselors, priests, pastors, etc. are unscripturally advising — "compromise."

Compromise is an unstable and weak solution to keep holding society together. As long as we continue to compromise we are doomed to a future of the bad fruits society now reaps. If we submit and become obedient, God will clean up the plagues in society, such as abortion. It will <u>not</u> be legislated out. It will be loved and obeyed out.

"I have always been one of those women who took offense to the Scripture 'Wives submit to your husbands.' I now know that for almost ten years I have been a rebellious wife. Many times I cried while reading this — the mistakes I have made, I cannot count them all. However, I take great comfort in knowing I can begin TODAY! And I have!"

A letter from
Antioch, California

CHAPTER TWENTY-FOUR

PEACE IS BANISHED FROM SOCIETY BECAUSE OF DISORDER. OUR LADY QUEEN OF PEACE COMES TO ESTABLISH ORDER, STARTING WITH MOTHERS, TO BRING PEACE

So we end up where we began, making a full circle, having now a much broader view. Viewing this subject as circling the tree at every step covers many points of view. We then must ask ourselves, "why?" Why is it that in a hospital nursery, ten babies can be before you with none of them harboring hatred or anger in their hearts, or the desire toward destructive behavior? Yes, children are born with certain characteristics which will affect their lives, but these characteristics can just as easily be taught and refined for good instead of evil as is the case so often in today's society. It is the parents who determine it. So much deception has taken place in order to mislead us and hinder us from discovering that the answer lies within the relationship of the mother and father. **satan understands that if we do not know the cause we cannot find the solution.** A kid's deviant behavior, such as the thirteen-year-old in handcuffs at the very beginning of this book, is blamed on everything but the real reason, which is **"defective parenting."** Poverty and a lack of education are the number one social blame and even believed to be a sin by some when, in fact, the money spent on the elimination of poverty and increasing education has not brought us closer to solving the problem. Rather, it has actually escalated and inflamed the problem. Remnants of the family structure physically survive financially by government aid, and so a provider (a father) is no longer needed or required. A great deal of education has promoted the destruction of the family unit, teaching also that man's mind can solve our problems, eliminating God completely.

This subject of poverty and education's influence on the family could be treated as another whole subject, going into much greater depth; but for the purpose of this writing, it can easily be covered by reflecting on Jesus' life. What of children raised in poverty, those with very little hope of higher education, housing so small that it is cramped even for three people, conditions so poor as to have to live without air conditioning, insufficient heating, no running water? This will not damage a child! For any one who has visited Joseph, Mary and Jesus' house in Loretto, Italy, can see that. It is very small, with poor heating and no air conditioning or running water. What damages a child is when there is no love, but instead strife between the husband and wife. The home

in which Jesus lived was turned into a palace, a royal household, by love and obedience. It easily surpassed any need for
higher education, because even though He was God, this education of love showed Him more than any institution could
have. About Jesus' being lost and then found by His parents
in the temple when He was twelve years old, Scripture states:

Luke 2: 51–52

"...Jesus for his part progressed steadily in
wisdom and age and grace before God and
men."

How was it, then, that Jesus, God Himself, was able to
progress steadily in wisdom and grace when He was being
guided by His parents, who were poor, and without having
higher education? Yes, Jesus received grace from the Father
in Heaven, but were not His earthly father and mother placed
by God to add grace and wisdom to Him by their love? All a
child needs to be whole is love and harmony between the two
parents. This is the major factor in the tragedy of the life of
the thirteen-year-old walking down a hallway in handcuffs.
It's the major and primary fruit of bad parenting, through the
violation of God's ordained order, which gives the example to
children to disobey, or if kept, to obey. While He **never**
sinned, Jesus Himself when only 12 years old, slipped away
somehow from His parents. Luke says Jesus remained be-

hind, unknown to His parents. His mother Mary, finding Him in the temple **three** days later, was so upset upon meeting Him She said, *"Son, why have you done this to us?!"* Scripture shows they had been searching for three days in grief and pain. Mary then tells her adolescent, with measured control, *"You see that your father and I have been searching for you in sorrow!"* In Luke 2:51, Scripture relates afterwards:

> **"Jesus went unto Nazareth and was obedient to his parents."**

The thirteen-year-old described in the beginning and the example of Jesus when he was twelve years old are in sharp contrast with each other. Yes, Jesus is God, but put that aside and view two adolescents of similar ages. Both had slipped away from their parents, but one became disobedient while the other became more obedient. It cannot be said Jesus was not tempted. He was more tempted than other teenagers because satan always wants to destroy holiness. But the difference was the parents, when viewing it on the **"human"** side.

One couple related a story:

> *"We were in a store recently and my wife started to go out the door only to be blocked by a little four-year-old playing in the doorway. My wife*

said politely to the little child, 'Be careful, you're going to get hurt,' to which he, not liking to be told what to do responded, 'I'm going to murder you.' It really made me angry and I wanted to discipline this little 'monster,' as what he needed was a good spanking. But then I stared in disbelief when he, as crudely as could be, pointed to someone smoking and said, 'Look, he's smoking a joint.' Right at this moment, I saw his mother, who couldn't care less and strutted out the door with more arrogance than an aircraft carrier could hold. Combining her attitude with her child's second comment made me realize this little 'monster' was born a lamb and what he had learned came through his parents or lack thereof. I felt sick and weakened to see such a little lamb being made into a goat."

Society is going to continue its downward spiral or be raised up, depending upon how parents live with each other. The following is reprinted from Caritas of Birmingham's July/December, 1993 Newsletter, originally taken from Maria Valtorta's **Poem of the Man-God**. Maria Valtorta related how Jesus spoke about His earthly father and His mother, Mary, and how their little home had everything even though He lived in poverty.

*"Not even now that I am in Heaven can I forget
the happy hours I spent beside Joseph, who, as if
he were playing with Me, guided Me to the point
of being capable of working. And when I look
at My putative father, I see once again the little
kitchen garden and the smoky workshop, and I
still appear to see Mother peep in with Her beautiful smile which turned the place into Paradise
and made us so happy.*

*"How much families should learn from the per-
fection of this couple who loved each other as
nobody else ever loved! Joseph was the head of
the family, and as such, his authority was undis-
puted and indisputable: before it, the Spouse and
Mother of God bent reverently and the Son of
God submitted Himself willingly. Whatever Joseph decided to do, was done well: there was no
discussion, no punctiliousness, no opposition.
His word was our little law. And yet, how much
humility there was in him! There never was any
abuse of power, or any decision against reason
only because he was the head of the family. His
Spouse was his sweet advisor. And if in Her
deep humility She considered Herself the servant
of Her consort, he drew from her wisdom of Full
of Grace, light to guide him in all events.*

"And I grew like a flower protected by vigorous trees, between those two loves that interlaced above Me, to protect Me, and love Me.

"No. As long as I was able to ignore the world because of My age, I did not regret being absent from Paradise. God the Father and the Holy Spirit were not absent, because Mary was full of Them. And the angels dwelt there, because nothing drove them away from that house. And one of them, I might say, had become flesh and was Joseph, an angelical soul freed from the burden of the flesh, intent only on serving God and His cause and loving Him as the Seraphim love Him. Joseph's look! It was as placid and pure as the brightness of a star unaware of worldly concupiscence. It was peace, and our strength.

"Many think that I did not suffer as a human being when the holy glance of the guardian of our home was extinguished by death. If I was God, and as such I was aware of the happy destiny of Joseph, and consequently I was not sorry for his death, because after, a short time in Limbo, I was going to open Heaven to him, as a Man I cried bitterly in the house now empty and deprived of his presence. I cried over My dead friend, and

should I not have cried over My holy friend, on whose chest I had slept when I was a little boy, and from whom I had received so much love in so many years?

"Finally I would like to draw the attention of parents to how Joseph made a clever workman of Me, without any help of pedagogical learning. As soon as I was old enough to handle tools, he did not let Me lead a life of idleness, but he started Me to work and he made use of My love for Mary as the means to spur Me to work. I was to make useful things for Mother. That is how he inculcated the respect which every son should have for his mother and the teaching for the future carpenter was based on that respectful and loving incentive.

"Where are now the families in which the little ones are taught <u>to love work as a means of pleasing their parents?</u> Children, nowadays, are the tyrants of the house. They grow hard, indifferent, ill-mannered towards their parents. They consider their parents as their servants, their slaves. They do not love their parents and they are scarcely loved by them. The 'reason' is that while you allow your children to become objec-

tionable, overbearing fellows, you become de-
tached from them with shameful indifference.

"They are everybody's children, except yours, O
parents of the twentieth century. They are the
children of the nurse, of the governess, of the col-
lege, if you are rich people. They belong to their
companions, they are the children of the streets,
of the schools, if you are poor. But they are not
yours. You, mothers, give birth to them and that
is all. And you, fathers, do exactly the same. But
a son is not only flesh. He has a mind, a heart, a
soul. Believe Me, no one is more entitled and
more obliged than a father and a mother to form
that mind, that heart, that soul.

"A family is necessary: it exists and must exist.
There is not theory or progress capable of de-
stroying this truth without causing ruin. A shat-
tered family can but yield men and women who
in future will be more perverted, and will cause
greater and greater ruin. And I tell you most so-
lemnly that it would be better if there were no
more marriages and no more children on the
earth, rather than have families less united than
the tribes of monkeys, families which are not
schools of virtue, of work, of love, of religion,

*but a babel in which everyone lives on his own
like disengaged gears, which end up by breaking.*

*"Broken families. You break up the most holy
way of social living and you see and suffer the
consequences. You may continue thus, if you so
wish. But do not complain if this world is becoming a deeper and deeper hell, a swelling place
of monsters who devour families and nations.
You want it. Let it be so."* [59]

Plainly put, the thirteen-year-old in handcuffs, along
with many youth in the world today, are not born that way.
The cause cannot be blamed on poverty, the lack of jobs, or
lack of education. It is the rejection of God's ordained order
which, once rejected, eliminates the possibility for love to
flourish. It has led to more and more dissension and hatred in
the family and in society. For where there is no love, hatred
will fill the void and dissension follows. Our Lady said on July 31, 1986:

**"Dear children, hatred gives birth to dissensions
and does not regard anyone or anything..."**

It is the time for fathers to obey God the Father, wives their
husbands, and children their parents. The battery to crank all
of this is the woman. She is to originate it through mother-

hood. Love and obedience is to be her only weapon. Her virtue will tame any harshness found in her husband, sons, and daughters. Without the wife's cooperation in this, the husband will never have the ability to direct and guide the "ship," the family, toward God. And if the husband refuses his responsibility in this, let it be the wife's meekness and purity that will shake his conscience rather than her lightning and thunder which inflames his wrath. For it is man who is completed by the woman, not she who is completed by the man. He was whole and out of him was taken the rib, making him incomplete, and she "a part" "of" him as well as "a part" "from" him is not complete until through wedlock they are again made one flesh. For out of one flesh came the woman. She was made for man, and man was made for God. It is by this order that they both became one before God, sharing equally His inheritance and grace.*

Harmony and peace must come back. It can only come and flourish in a sound structure with a center solidly in order. We quoted William Yates in the beginning as saying:

*"Things fall apart — the center cannot hold —
mere anarchy is loose upon the world."*

---

* Religious vocations do the same in their offering in holy wedlock to Christ through the consecration of their lives to Him, and all of these writings apply to them equally as well as to married couples.

In a book written in the year 1889 appears a quote from Lambert on what the world would be like without obedience. It was a prophecy for the world at the end of the 19th century and is proof of what happens when obedience disappears:

> *"What would become of the world without obedience? What is more necessary than this virtue to maintain order and discipline? Experience has proved this.* <u>*Where obedience is not observed, there can be nothing but trouble; disorder glides in, and peace is banished.*</u>

> *"A disunited whole is threatened with destruction, and ruin is unavoidable. But, on the contrary, where obedience is kept, all will be edified. In noticing this perfect unanimity one would see that these contented minds are perfectly united. If there can be anything lasting on earth, it is when it is united, and when everything is in perfect order, and this can never be the case where obedience is not strictly observed."*

Over 100 years later, we today know now what that world without obedience is like. We must now get on our knees, rectify and repent, and do what Our Lady has said so many times:

"Pray, Pray, Pray."

We end with the rest of Our Lady's message of July 31, 1986, already quoted above. It contains the essence of all that has been written, and makes a full circle around this subject from most every point of view. It should be meditated upon with great depth and prayer. What has been written in many pages, Our Lady, in Her wisdom, says only in one paragraph:

July 31, 1986:

> **"Dear children, hatred gives birth to dissensions and does not regard anyone or anything. I call you always to bring harmony and peace. Especially, dear children, in the place where you live, act with love. Let your only instrument always be love. By love turn everything into good which satan desires to destroy and possess. Only that way will you be completely mine and I shall be able to help you. Thank you for having responded to my call."**

Our love goes out to all of you. We sympathize with your struggles, and our hearts are laden many times with your sorrows. Be strong, have courage, and face the enemy with a firm decision. Do not be weak in your resolve to be one of Our Lady's children, for it means trials. As the angels who appear with Our Lady cry when Our Lady does, we Her children also cry. But there are other times, we must also remember, when Our Lady is joyful, so it is that the angels are the same and we, too, as Her children share that same joy. God bless you!

The following is a continuing chapter of the previous writings and is a "<u>must read</u>."

PART TWO

UNMASKING SATAN'S PLANS

"Both my husband and I just recently have been confused as to why our parish priest is using humankind, people, brothers <u>and</u> sisters, etc. instead of mankind, men, just brothers, and when it changes actual Bible readings it certainly seems wrong!

"Also, for years I wanted to have my husband take his role as <u>head</u> of our family — the father of our children and of our home. Now after many years of prayer, I am happy to read in your book that that is the way Our Lord wants the family to be. Now when my girlfriends call me '<u>door-mat</u>' to my husband, I will only respond with — 'it's time you read the Bible and become your husband's wife and truly make a <u>home</u> for your family.'"

A letter from
Hancock, Michigan

CHAPTER TWENTY-FIVE

SATAN EXPOSED

Our Lady's messages have led to the unmasking of satan's agenda, his plans and tactics. The following few pages will be of great benefit for wisdom in understanding the true agenda of what may seem to be good, but has resulted in bad fruit and will continue to do so. A prayer to the Holy Spirit now would aid you greatly in understanding what you are about to read.

Sadly, we are now living in a time when there is a reversal of roles or, at least, the neutralizing of man's role, more specifically the father's role. Many signs point to what seems to be an agenda for the feminization of men or, at the very least, the neutralizing of man's guidance. Manly traits, such as chivalry, protecting, providing, honor, etc. are not necessarily viewed as qualities to attain. In saying this, we do not speak of manly traits which are uncivilized, rather those of dignity and honor, of denying self and of leading. We are now developing a society in which not just teenage boys are wearing earrings but men as well! These signs are the feminization of men and are a sign of sickness, of disorder. Where are the men who are setting the example against this — that this is not something men do? The influence of the feminine is out of balance and spilling out into male identity. Boys and men have lost a great deal of their identity, and many are confused as to who they are and what their roles are. They are scared to be too strong in leadership, fearing they will offend the radical thoughts of those who place women's authority on an equal with men. This thought now prevails even among many Christian women today who would not consider or describe themselves as radical.

H.B. London, whom we quoted earlier in the previous writings, said in his interview:

> *Q: What kind of influence does the woman have on children?*

> A: **There are startling statistics... (that) where we are going is to be a female-driven society in many ways, where the influence on the children is going to be almost completely a female influence. According to George Barnan, the researcher,...by the years 2000 – 2010, 80 percent of all ethnic children will be born to unwed mothers; anglo children — 40 percent to unwed mothers. The role of**

the father is going to be increasingly more
important."[60]

This process of feminization exists and is a clear depar-
ture from the Scriptures. How is it that we change the very
ways and references that God Himself has inspired? For instance, the Scriptures refer to the angels as "he." God's holy
word gives them the male gender in terms of reference to
them. It's not to say whether they are male or female. The
point is that God refers to them as a manly being.

Rev 7:2

> *I saw another "angel" come up from the east,*
> *holding the seal of the Living God. "He" cried*
> *out at the top of "his" voice to the four angels*
> *who were given power to ravage the land and*
> *sea.*

How can it be reconciled that today many are referring to angels as "she?" Where does their authority come from to do
such a thing? There is no opinion expressed here. It is clearly
rooted in the Scriptures that angels are referred to as the male
gender.

There are many other signs that support these observa-
tions, but one in particular we will look at in depth is the

changing of traditional words and the rearranging of the gender order. You will hear many times now from the altar instead of "brothers and sisters," the exact reversal, "my sisters and brothers..." This turn from the tradition, from how it has always been said, is obviously in contrast to the parallel found in the beginning — first the man (brother), Adam, and second the woman, (sister) Eve. This reverse is reflective of the reversal of roles promoted by those whose human agenda is to change man and woman's position and their roles. It is a "tearing down," rather than what would be proposed as a "building up." "Sisters and brothers" is a clear agenda and not reflective of God's order. This change of language is so subtle as to be almost as nothing, yet is part of a plan to change society socially as well as to change men and women's roles. satan is very much a part of it, and it will lead to a furthering of the separation of man and woman. satan always labels his agendas the opposite of what really is the truth. At any bar that has "Happy Hour," you will find very lonely and sad people. They are not happy, but everyone pretends to be. Psychiatrists tell us the homosexual population is the top group for suicides, unfulfilled lives, depression, etc., yet satan captures the name "gay," painting a picture of a carefree life, good, fun, joyful, when, in fact, it is a life of misery.

Now we have a nicely packaged name called "inclusive language" which supposedly is to include men and women and not promote social injustice; at least that is what we are led to believe. When, in fact, it is just like the other terms already given as examples, a play to disguise, an agenda to divide. Inclusive language is a by-product of woman's challenging man's authority. It is no longer content with just equal authority, but now wants to rule man, which is the real agenda and what satan desires. Inclusive language, at the very least, is highly discriminatory, separating, and divisive. It implies and tries to tell us that to say "woman," "man," "boy," "girl" is unnecessary and dividing when one word has always been "inclusive" of everyone. The words "man," "mankind," "all men" include all women, all boys, all girls, together in unity with the human family. Individuals who segregate them under the deceptive disguise of the "fairness" of inclusive language are actually leading to disunion, which results in the furthering of the deterioration of society by creating an environment for the jockeying of power between the two genders, when what God intended is oneness as mankind. No one is asking why we must suddenly come up with a new word when we already have one which already includes everyone — "mankind." It is very plain that there is an objection of all people coming under the word "man"kind. Anyone with a little logic can see a clear attack against male authority. The word "human"kind is the product of social engineering to change that which God has established. Our Lady in Medjugorje does not conform to these plans of man to orchestrate society's thinking. Our Lady says:

January 2, 1989

> **"My dear children,...I want you to become,
> dear children, my announcers and my sons who
> will bring peace, love, conversion..."**

Can anyone dare say Our Lady is against women by saying **"my sons"**? Is She sexist, chauvinistic? Does Our Lady exclude daughters because She only says "sons"? Hardly! Our Lady, as Mother and Queen in Heaven, is the ultimate in "inclusive" of all. "Sons" means also daughters, little boys, girls, and also adults, men and women — a lot of different groups all in one little word **"<u>sons.</u>"** It is as inclusive as you can get. Is this an isolated statement of Our Lady? No, because other times Our Lady has only said "brothers" in referring to both men and women:

February 2, 1984

> **"Pray, because I need more prayers. Be reconciled, because I desire reconciliation among you
> and more love for each other, <u>like brothers</u>. I
> wish that prayer, peace, and love bloom in you."**

...and again...

January 23, 1986

> "Dear children, again I call you to prayer with
> the heart. If you pray with the heart, dear child-
> ren, <u>the ice of your brothers' hearts</u> will melt
> and every barrier shall disappear. Conversion
> will be easy for all who desire to accept it. You
> must pray for this gift which by prayer you must
> obtain for your "<u>neighbor</u>." Thank you for hav-
> ing responded to my call."

...and more recently ..

April 25, 1995

> "Dear children! Today I call you to love. Little
> children, without love you cannot live, neither
> with God <u>nor with brother</u>. Therefore, I call all
> of you to open your hearts to the love of God
> that is so great and open to each one of you..."

Can it be possible Our Lady only means males when
She says brothers? If you accept that, how do you reconcile
later in the January 23, 1986 message above when Our Lady
refers to these same "brothers" as "neighbors"? Are our
neighbors all male? Our Lady's words are inclusive of "sisters" in the messages above. The language we have had has

been <u>inclusive</u> and just as we now have terms like happy hour, gay, "pal"amony, etc., we have the term "inclusive language" to disguise its real agenda. The present "inclusive language" is not inclusive at all, rather its purpose is to exclude and separate. In the book, **Let Me Be A Woman**, the author, Elizabeth Elliot writes:

> *"I have come to treat the word 'person' rather gingerly in recent years because it is so overused. I hear people talk of wanting to be treated 'not as a woman but as a human being,' or 'as a person.' I hear words like 'chairperson' and 'spokesperson,' and even absurdities such as the 'freshperson class,' and 'personhole covers (manhole covers).' There is something seriously distorted about this view of humanity. I don't want anybody treating me as a 'person'* __rather__ *than as a woman. Our sexual differences are the terms of our life, and to obscure them in any way is to weaken the very fabric of life itself. When they are lost, we are lost. Some women fondly imagine a new beginning of liberty, but it is in reality a new bondage, more bitter than anything they seek to be liberated from.*

> *"I want to know not 'people' but men and women. I am interested in men as men, in women as*

*women, and when you marry you marry a man
because he is a man, and being a man he becomes your husband. This is the glory of marriage — two separate and distinct kinds of beings
are unified.*" [61]

The word "mankind" signifies both genders. It actual
ly identifies male and female; that is, its meaning, while the
supposed goal of saying "personhood" or "humankind" is
supposed to do that. Rather, it actually lowers identity to that
of a species: no genders — one kind, almost animal.

What fruit has inclusive language shown or will it
show? The challenge of traditional wording is an attack on
God's authority. Marija, the visionary from Medjugorje, was
asked by a priest: *"Marija, what do I tell nuns who are saying
God is a woman?"* Marija, looking straight into his face said:
"God is our Father who art in Heaven." The priest, taken ab-
ack said: *"Oh! I never thought of that answer!"* We have experienced bad fruit with the loss of respect for God the Father
and will continue this loss as these plans become more prevalent. Fruit is the test and with a little wisdom, one can see it
has led to separation, not unity.

Indeed, God is our Father. Jesus is the Son. Both
their spirits are the Holy Spirit, all in one. As one good, holy
priest said, *"The very being of God represents masculinity,"*

through which comes femininity, just as Eve came from
Adam. Within the Trinity is the key to how femininity is to
be in union with masculinity. Author Elizabeth Elliot writes:

*"We know that this order of rule and submission
is descended from the nature of God Himself.
Within the Godhead there is both the just and legitimate authority of the Father and the willing
and joyful submission of the Son. From the union of the Father and the Son proceeds a third
personality, (being) the Holy Spirit, (in the same
way), the personality of a marriage proceeds
from the one flesh which is established from the
union of two separate personalities.*

*"Here, in the reflection of the nature of the Trini-
ty in the institution of marriage, is the key to the
definition of masculinity and femininity. The
image of God could not be fully reflected without
the elements of rule, submission, and union."* [62]

How can it be accepted that "today's thought" that women of yester-year were enslaved and degraded, when, in fact, they were held in such high esteem, virtue, and fondness that from the past we refer many terms of the highest honor to the female gender.

The "Mother" Church — Pope John Paul II writes in his 1995 encyclical "Consecrated Life":

"The whole Church finds in 'her' hands this great gift and gratefully devotes 'her self' to promoting it with respect......"

Another time the Pope writes of the Church:

"for it eloquently expresses 'her' inmost nature as 'bride'."

— Ships are referred to as "she". "Look at her sailing. She's magnificent!"
— "She's a grand ole flag."
— There is no one who does not love nature as it is affectionately called "mother" nature.
— "Mother" homeland.

One of the highest dignities referred to with the woman gender is Wisdom. The Bible itself calls Wisdom "Her"/"She". In Sirach 51:13–14 it states:

"When I was young and innocent, I sought wisdom. 'She' came to me in "her" beauty and until the end I will cultivate "her".

As we know, The Virgin Mary, Herself, "is" Wisdom and "Her" position, with the exception of Jesus, is <u>above</u> every male who has ever been born.

With this in mind, the cry today to be equal in authority with man requires women to step down from their regal throne of aspiring to imitate Our Lady to that lower level of male authority which must compete in the work place, struggling to outperform male counterparts in their effort to constantly survive. In this world of the work place, attributes such as sweetness, kindness, gentleness, etc., are often crushed. A woman, who follows and lowers herself to a man's role, loses those attributes which are a cause for her elevation and admiration. They lose all that which makes womanhood special and the reasons why men held women in higher esteem, even above themselves in past times, rather than the role women now hold in society. The role today's woman holds can be easily defined through a glance at any magazine cover. As one looks at any of these covers of magazines, is what they portray worthy of the title "woman" or "mother?" Yet all the above points of a woman's dignity comes through respect of fathers, through respecting God the Father and His title.

262

CHAPTER TWENTY-SIX

IN RESPECT OF GOD "THE" "FATHER"

$\mathbf{A}$ letter confronting the facade of inclusive language follows. It was written to a priest, who is basically opposed to inclusive language, and it was slipped in during the readings at Sunday Mass without his knowledge:

Dear Father,   *November 14, 1995*

"On Sunday, September 24, you celebrated the 8:30 a.m. Mass. The lector read the Readings. Reading the Book of 1 Timothy 2:1–8, he read the words "all men." To my surprise, he then added the words "that is everyone." The next two times he was supposed to read "<u>all men</u>," he changed it and read the word "everyone" in its place, completely dropping the biblical transla-tion. My concerns follow.

"'All men' is inclusive of all men, women, child-ren, etc. Changing it to "everyone" does not cla-rify the meaning any further since there already

is a universal understanding that "all men"
means "everyone" in the English language. So
there can be no arguments put forth to change
"all men," because it is already inclusive rather
than "exclusive" as some would try to portray.

"I can only conclude that those who put forth the
agenda to change these words, place before us a
disguise, a "façade" of justice and fairness to lead
us to think that by doing so they include rather
than exclude, all of which seems fair and allows
this agenda to slide by the members of the church
without alarm to the real intent. How, by chang-
ing wording, can we suddenly include something
which has never been excluded? That being the
case proves that this agenda is not concerned
with women being included, rather their problem
is the structure of authority which is signified and
confirmed when we say "men," when applied to
all women, boys, and girls.

"It seems clear to me that many are seduced into
accepting these changes, thinking this is justice;
we are "righting wrongs against women." How-
ever, little wisdom is put forth to connect its real
agenda, which is an attack on male authority,
and once this is achieved, the deterioration of so-

ciety follows because of no solid direction. This is because direction is God-ordained and in the hands of the male, the provider, and if his importance is nullified, society will lose its way. It can only be this in-depth reason since saying "men," when applied to all people, is as inclusive as you can get. It then becomes obvious that the real reason, the in-depth reason, is the rejection of "man's" biblical mandate to guide and lead. This attack on male authority, this rejection, has led to the lack of importance of the father in the family. He is no longer the guide, rather an equal vote with his wife and now even his children. However, also with this erosion of fatherhood has come the challenging of having only male priests, resentment against the hierarchy of the Church, and the questioning of it. Still, this is not the end desire of the agenda. It is apparent that the ultimate goal of this language game is the restructuring and social re-engineering of male authority with the expressed purpose to alter society in order to weaken man's (male) authority, which will weaken God's authority, the latter being "the" ultimate goal of this agenda. All authority being from God is, of course, always resisted by those forces against God. The weaken-

ing of fatherhood has resulted in the parallel of the weakening of God the Father's fatherhood in society. God the Father is no longer respected just as fathers are not. God's ordained authority is sacred. Men need not apologize for exercising that which God gave them nor be timid in using it, for God expects it when put into action with love or to keep His commandments.

"It must be reflected upon that Eve was deceived. Adam was not. Eve was deceived by the serpent and obeyed him. Adam was seduced by the woman and obeyed her. Authority flowed from God to Adam, and he was to listen to the Father's commands. It was he who was told before Eve was created not to eat of the fruit. Eve, obeying Adam, told the serpent that they were not to eat of the fruit. The commands from God passed through the man's authority to the woman and the woman expressed it to the serpent. She did not listen to her husband and did not submit to his guidance which came from the Heavenly Father. Eve, being deceived, reversed the order of authority and listened to the serpent, obeying him. Adam knew it was wrong yet followed the woman, obeying her. Today, it is the same. We are becoming a female-driven society. The dan-

ger is women are inclined to being deceived while men have a natural ability to know the right direction, even if they don't follow it.

"Women are a touch of God, offering great enhancement to man and the elevation of society. Woman was made for man. Man was made for God. She is man's helpmate, both through which God is glorified. This is supported in Scripture which states:

1 Corinthians 11:7–10

"A man is the image of God and the reflection of His glory. Woman, in turn, is the reflection of man's glory. Man was not made from woman but woman from man. Neither was man created for woman but woman for man."

"The danger is when positions of authority are filled by women on a wide scale, the degradation of society will follow. Women have the "qualities" to fill these positions, even exceeding men in many ways. But they do not possess the direction, guideship ability, and far-reaching consequences of decisions made that come with God-

given authority in the same way a man has. A mechanic can easily mislead a woman about a problem with her car that does not exist, because it is her nature to trust. Man is more suspect and can be misled but far less likely than women. From satan's standpoint, therefore, it becomes important, if evil is to prevail, that man's authority be not only challenged but usurped which, in turn, will lead to the destruction of society. Once a great many positions of authority are filled with women, by **usurpation,** *society's fall will follow, just as Eve's trust in the serpent began the fall of all men. While I do not argue that women can fill positions and exercise authority, it must come through man and be subject to him, not equal to or over him.* * *Through this she will be protected and fruit will come from her wisdom and decisions. When not subject to man, she is destined to go astray and will be deceived. Even saints understanding this value, so as not to go astray, protected themselves by a spiritual director, submitting to spiritual direction.*

---

* This has nothing to do with her equality in regard to worth and dignity as a woman. Before God as a soul, she is equally entitled to the same dignity and graces due a man, nor is woman any less, even in the slightest, in comparison to man in these regards.

"St. Teresa herself spoke about women and how easily they are deceived. She spoke of evil among the religious and said she speaks more of women than of men. Carmelite Kieran Kavanaugh O.C.D., author of St. Teresa of Avila's four volumes of her life, writes:

> **"The ideal gradually grew more widespread that women, the daughters of Eve, could serve as satan's intermediary, in order to more easily tempt man and draw him to evil."**

"I know what I say to you would be perceived by present society as radical, yet I know past Christian societies would judge the present society as radical. I prefer to be in harmony with those principals which, when followed, cause society to function in an orderly way. Anyone who prays, studies the lives of the saints, the Scriptures, Our Lady's messages given in Medjugorje, and the Church's past history will come to the same conclusions.

"While I deserve it because of my sins, I, as an individual, do not mind my manhood, husbandhood, and fatherhood being demeaned, de-

graded, and trampled. However, because my manhood, husbandhood, and fatherhood are characteristic representation on earth of God the Father's to my children, my wife, and society, I revolt against what in truth is a 'masked' attack on God our Father. I encourage all 'males' to resist, through love, the softening and mushing of that which is God-given and to remain firm in the exercising of their rightful authority from God for family and society. It is time for them to fill their sacred and holy position which can only be done by living His precepts, and then for them to realize the importance of this authority in their roles to lead society back on course. It is not important that society no longer gives the 'male' this authority, for it is not they who decide it nor theirs to give. We have it by God's design. We should exercise it even against a society which rejects it. It is we who have the strength and right to do so because it is from Him Who, being the singular author of all men, is the "One" from Whom all authority rests.

"I, therefore, most vehemently oppose the change of Scriptural words, especially to meet an agenda of social rearranging. I know many of those who do, do so without even realizing what they are

*doing. It is important that they be made aware. I
know to say things such as this is not wise by the
world's ways if anyone is concerned about repu-
tations and what people may think of him.
However, Jesus' example of not going with the
prevailing thought, but rather speaking clearly, is
the road to travel. No doubt that it was for Him
very rough, but so too will it be for any who
takes up the cross, tries to live the faith, and
speaks clearly. I am not thin-skinned, rather I
place the armor of Jesus before me as protection.
Whatever you choose to do with this I leave to
you. Whether you use it, post it in the Church, or
discard it, I trust in God your direction for it."*

In Jesus, Mary, and Joseph,
A Friend of Medjugorje

The truth is through many plans of satan, inclusive language being one, the Fatherhood of God is being undermined. Why? It
is important for satan to attack God's authority in order for him
to change men and women's roles here on earth.

One priest mentioned on Father's Day that at a detention home he visits he cannot mention God the Father because the juveniles have no earthly father to relate to and, in
most cases, hate the name. That same view for them holds

true for the Father in Heaven. Fathers' and mothers' roles are extremely important and we must make them more clear in the future and resist the whims of social changes. We must resist this social engineering. Indeed, satan's goal is to make God the Father hated and so satan works to make earthly fatherhood despised and hated, which serves perfectly his plan.

Today's society clearly suffers from this challenge to male authority and the father's right to lead the family. Few wives understand this, as in the case of the following couple:

> *"A couple was in counseling sessions and a question was put forth to them. The wife said, 'I'll do whatever my husband says. He is my husband. Whatever he says that is what I'll do.' Upon which she then got up, turned to him, and said, 'Get up Bill. Come on. Let's go!'"*

It was quite obvious to the counselor who was in charge, that the woman lived not at all what she professed.

Present society's problems may be blamed on many things; music, husband's abandonment, divorce, crime etc... While these are great problems in our society today, just as many would blame the problems of Israel and the Arab countries on many different issues, they are not the **root** problem. They are the "fruit" of the core root problem. The Arabs and

Jews' core root problem was Sarah's usurping and Abraham's allowing Sarah to lead him. Few realize today when they hear about the conflict between the Jews and Arabs that it originates from a family problem dating back thousands of years, in which Sarah did not obey, but usurped Abraham's authority, and he complied, allowing her to lead him. At the prodding of his wife, he had relations with a servant who gave birth to a son, "Ishmael." Later, Sarah conceived and gave birth to Isaac. Ishmael and Isaac were family, related by blood, yet through Sarah's bending and usurping, hatred entered the family, and Isaac, whom all Jews descended from and Ishmael, whom all Arabs descended from, set the stage for thousands of years of suffering, sorrow, and persecutions, all because of a single act of disobedience to God's structure and working order.

Still it might be said, "But I'm not Sarah. My small acts account for nothing." Sarah certainly did not understand the importance of her role at the time she was living. How could she? In the present time, the time we all are living in, Our Lady, in Her first message to the world, had this to tell us:

January 25, 1987

"...Dear children, I want you to comprehend that God has chosen each one of you, in order to use you in a great plan for the salvation of

mankind. You are not able to comprehend how great your role is in God's design..."

By this we see that a woman, living out her role as wife and mother as perfectly as possible, **"will,"** not **"may,"** have a "great" effect upon society and the world.

Today the hatred between Israel and the Arab countries is blamed on land squabbles, atrocities against each other, etc...which is a distortion of the reason all those issues exist. In comparison, the core problem in today's society is the struggle for female domination over male authority and also man's weakness to hold the course which he knows in his heart he must follow to guide the family.

Just as satan hid the Arab and Jew problem beneath conflict and strife, so today he also does the same between men and women, by raising issues of conflict and strife, all of which are the result of jockeying for power, and all of which would be alleviated with only "one" head. Through conflict and strife satan is able to keep us from discovering and going deep enough to see the problem. satan, then, is easily able to perpetuate it.

Yet, with a little wisdom satan's deception can be uncovered, and there is evidence of this everywhere in society. Usually the best and most clear evidence of satan's hidden

agenda of reversing the roles set down by God can be found
associated with vices. Cigarette advertising is extremely guilty
of this influence on society, even for those who do not smoke.
Its message still influences subliminally. A current Newport
cigarette advertisement on billboards and airport displays
shows a man and a woman arm wrestling. His muscles are
flexed and his face is tilted downward with a grimace on it as
he looks at his large muscle. The woman is looking outward
towards the public with a somewhat devious smile, as if to say,
"I've got him under my control," effortlessly holding him at
bay. His countenance seems to say, "I am not strong enough.
My muscles are much larger, and she is a woman. How is it
she dominates me?" He seems puzzled at the loss of his manhood. She conveys in her countenance, "Women are in
charge; use your womanly traits to dominate. Everything is in
my control. Look at me! I'm happy being in charge of man.
You can be the same." Are we reading more than what is
there? Study the picture! One might say, "Should we really
believe satan is active in such advertising?" Yes! It is a promotion of a vice. When this is the case, satan is very active in
such promotion. He has a master scheme with multiple purposes, and smoking is not his sole message. We must ask ourselves what arm wrestling between a man and a woman has to
do with cigarettes, unless its message is much more than cigarettes. Stranger still, a cigarette does not even appear in the
ad. Another recent cigarette company shows a woman and

man both wearing pants with a statement saying to the effect, "Who cares who wears the pants?" — a clear challenge of manly authority.

Can it then be said that all these people who write these advertisements have a set agenda to alter society? No. While some do, many have no clue as to the under- lying agen- da of sa- tan. There is fertile ground amongst vice for

satan to inspire in the promotion of any vice that requires tal- ent to be creative, to be inspired, or to think up ideas. It would be incorrect to think that satan would not be aggres- sively involved. Just as with an open chicken coop and a fox, satan **will** inspire. There are so many things, so many ideas that we buy ourselves that we know are harmful to us both physically and spiritually. Why, then, do we buy them? Be- cause they are packaged in such an irresistible and enticing way. More than the "thing," we "accept" the "message" they are selling. Our Lady warned us about this on June 25, 1989, at Ivanka's annual apparition. She said:

> **"Pray, because you are in great temptation and danger because the world and material goods lead you into slavery. satan is active in this plan..."**

So, can satan's activity in inspiring these thoughts to put forth his agenda be discounted? This breeding ground for evil reveals many things. Not long ago a massive billboard campaign, again on cigarettes, had this as its promotional line, "Your Basic Message." Is anyone logically able to show what this has to do with cigarettes? On the other hand, it has a great deal to do with an assault on Our Lady's messages. Our Lady's messages are simple, given for Her children in a very uncomplicated way, for us to be as children to understand them. Her "basic message" is to offer us holiness. satan's basic message is to offer us vice, pleasure, entertainment, etc..., especially for youth, which is cigarettes in this case, but often times many other things as well. Jakov was quoted as saying once that Our Lady gives us the "basic messages" of **prayer, fasting, confession, peace.**

Of course, these examples begin to rise into the issues and away from the core problem, but they are offered to show you how much satan has infiltrated throughout our daily lives

and to reveal his hidden agenda to divert you from recogniz-
ing a problem and finding the solution, which is to follow
God's structure for the family. Many things in society reveal
step by step the "equal authority" agenda and its aim to "ups-
tage" all male authority. All that is needed is a little observa-
tion of entities like the media, teaching institutions, government, etc....observation which will easily reveal a massive,
masterful, interwoven plan of which none of the mentioned
entities sit down and plan together, yet all are influenced by
an unseen, evil force which causes these entities to work in
union together for the same agenda. Only one being can do
that. lucifer.

The saying, "Hell hath no fury like a woman scorned"
is hardly recalled today, in order that no one will be reminded
of the hell which will come into a family when a wife and
mother usurps her husband's authority. We wipe away and
sanitize all reminders of such so that in doing so, rebellion
against a husband or disobeying him will appear as no big
deal. Any reminder that would bring attention to certain
truths, such as the previous saying, is looked on in our present
society with disdain. Hence, the naming of hurricanes using
women's names solely, which had been done for decades,
stopped. The reason put forth was a "fairness" which equates
that everything must be equal between men and women, even
though God did not make it that way, either physically or
emotionally. Yet in this case the truth is very simple. State-

ments such as "Hell hath no fury like a woman scorned" (hurricane), even though they speak truth, are labeled as "no-nos." satan wants to hide these reminders and he tricks us in many ways. He plays on our sensitivity for fairness, our language, our sayings, our directions, which easily causes us to place ourselves in his hands. We do not reflect on why we are changing the gender names of hurricanes. Why were they named only after women to start with? Was it because there were elements of truth that all of society knew and accepted of how a rebellious women's disposition compared to a hurricane? Our changing it insinuates that those who began calling hurricanes women's names were wrong, that there was no true reason for naming hurricanes as such. The purpose in originally naming hurricanes <u>was</u> because of the truth that what a rebellious woman is like is comparable to a hurricane. The purpose of this example is not to name hurricanes after women but to unveil this one among hundreds of other slight things which are master-minded by the forces of evil to deceive or to conceal certain realities. We must **<u>reflect</u>** on all these things and not accept them and put ourselves in satan's hands. Our Lady said May 25, 1987:

> **"...Dear children, you are ready to commit sin, and put yourselves in the hands of satan without reflecting..."**

It certainly is not a sin, and it may not be a big deal to you about changing the gender names of hurricanes. You may be glad that it has happened, and that is not wrong in itself. However, what is important is the "reason" this and hundreds of other issues are going in this direction — that satan is playing with us. He is misguiding and misdirecting our souls through seemingly trivial things, but once reflected upon show up as sparks which light the forest fires. Our Lady says:

> **"...satan is playing with you and with your souls..."** (March 25, 1992)

Also Our Lady says:

> **"...Dear children, satan is lurking for each individual. Especially in everyday affairs, he wants to spread confusion among each one of you..."** (September 4, 1986)

There is no practical way to resist society's direction in changing language, gender roles, etc. except through the living of Our Lady's messages and the enlightening of souls, one by one. Tell them and encourage them to read these writings and pray. Pray to Our Lady, that many more will come to the truth Her messages are now revealing and exposing for <u>today.</u>

We are very much interested in how this book has affected your life and/or others around you. Your experiences may help in encouraging others in overcoming their hardships or even preventing them altogether. There has been much fruit produced in peoples' lives through this sort of correspondence in the past. If you would please write down your experiences and send your letters to:

Caritas of Birmingham
c/o "How to Change Your Husband"
100 Our Lady Queen of Peace Drive
Sterrett, Alabama 35147 USA

Thank you

* * * * * * * * * * * *

The important writings you have just read will convict and change society. Our goals must be to spread these truths. How to Change Your Husband, originally printed in the Community of Caritas of Birmingham newsletter, is now being made available in book form at a price in volume discount in order for you to permeate society with the truth, in order to change it. You may order in discounted volume to give to a friend, spouse, children, or give away at churches and conferences.

You may purchase this book at your local bookstore. If they do not have it, please ask them to order it. In that way, distribution will spread and many more will be led to Our Lady's plans to change the world through the family.

Buy at your local bookstore. If not available, you may order from: Caritas of Birmingham, 100 Our Lady Queen of Peace Drive, Sterrett, Alabama 35147 USA or call (205) 672-2000, ext. 315. You may use Visa, Mastercard, or Discover.

How to Change Your Husband Owner's Manual for the Family BF103		
(Check One)		
☐ 1	$6.00	
☐ 5	$20.00	($4.00EA)
☐ 10	$30.00	($3.00EA)
☐ 25	$47.50	($1.90EA)
☐ 50	$90.00	($1.80EA)
☐ 100	$170.00	($1.70EA)
☐ 1000	$1400.00	($1.40EA)

Shipping & Handling

Order Sub-total	U.S. Mail (Standard)	UPS (Faster)
$0-$10.00	$5.00	$9.00
$10.01-$20.00	$7.50	$11.50
$20.01-$50.00	$10.00	$14.00
$50.01-$100.00	$15.00	$19.00
Over $100.00	15% of total	18% of total

For overnight delivery, call for pricing.
***International (Surface):**
Double above shipping Cost.
Call for faster International delivery.

Endnotes for the book "Owner's Manual for the Family"/"How to Change Your Husband"

1 Shelby County Probation Officer of Alabama
2 Bishop Fulton Sheen, Retreat for Priests, Loyola Retreat House, Potomac, MD, February, 1972.
3 Jan Connell, The Visions of the Children, St. Martin's Press, © 1992, p. 148.
4 Homily given in Catholic Church in Jacksonville, Florida.
5 "Encyclical on Christian Marriage of Pius XI," St. Paul Book and Media.
6 Homily given at Our Lady of the Valley Catholic Church in Birmingham, Alabama by Father Mike MacMahon.
7 "Family Voice" Magazine, January, 1995
8 Elizabeth Rice Handford, Me? Obey Him?, Sword of the Lord Publishers, © 1994, p. 35.
9 Ibid., p. 50 & 78
10 Father Paul Wickens, "Handbook For Parents, Common Sense Rules for Catholic Mothers and Fathers." Newmann Publication, p. 16.
11 "Encyclical on Christian Marriage of Pius XI," St. Paul Book and Media, p.37.
12 "The Catholic Hearth," quote by Cardinal Griffin, May, 1995, Vol, 3, No. 6, p. 46
13 "Encyclical on Christian Marriage of Pius XI," St. Paul Book and Media.
14 Ibid.
15 Talk given by Ivan to pilgrims in Medjugorje, August, 1994.
16 "Encyclical on Christian Marriage of Pius XI," St. Paul Book and Media.
17 Associated Press, Birmingham News, August 14, 1995.
18 Shelby County Probation Officer of Alabama.
19 Rev. T. Dewitt Talmage, D.D., Pathway of Life, the Christian Herald, © 1888, p. 457.
20 Ibid., p. 459.
21 Ibid., p. 463.
22 Anne Husted Burleigh, Journey Up The River, Ignatius Press, © 1994, p. 46.
23 Wendy Leifeild, Mother of the Saints, Servant Publication, © 1991, pp. 77-88.
24 Ibid., pp. 77-88.
25 Wife, Mother, Mystic - The Story of Anna Maria Taigi.
26 St. Francis De Sales, An Introduction to The Devout Life, TAN Books and Publishers.
27 Ibid.
28 Elizabeth Rice Handford, Your Clothes Say It for You, Sword of the Lord Publishers, © 1976, pp. 59-61.
29 Shelby County Probation Officer of Alabama.
30 Maria Valtorta, Poem of the Man-God, Volume 4, Centro Editoriale Valtortiano, © 1990, pp. 37–38.
31 Ibid., p. 281.
32 Ibid., p. 212.
33 Father Paul Wickens, "Handbook for Parents, Common Sense Rules for Catholic Mothers and Fathers" Newmann Publishers, p. 15.

34 "Webster's New Collegiate Dictionary", G. & C. Merrim Company, © 1980.

35 Maria Valtorta, Poem of the Man-God, Volume 4, Centro Editoriale Valtortiano, © 1990, p. 211.

36 James Dobson, "Focus On the Family Newsletter", Feb., 1995.

37 Phone interview with "Focus On the Family's" H.B. London.

38 "Liguorian Magazine", June, 1995, p.6.

39 Phone interview with "Focus On the Family's" H.B. London.

40 Taken from a letter sent to Caritas.

41 Taken from a letter sent to Caritas.

42 James Dobson, "Focus On the Family Newsletter", Feb., 1995.

43 Rev. T. Dewitt Talmage, D.D., Pathway of Life, The Christian Herald, © 1888, p. 467.

44 Ibid., p. 471.

45 Ibid., p. 451.

46 Maria Valtorta, Poem of the Man-God, Volume 4, Centro Editoriale Valtortiano, © 1990, p. 213.

47 Dee Jepson, Jesus Called Her Mother, Bethany House Publishing, © 1992, p. 149.

48 Maria Valtorta, Poem of the Man-God, Volume 4, Centro Editoriale Valtortiano, © 1990, p. 213.

49 Jan Connell, The Visions of the Children, St. Martin's Press, © 1992, p. 177.

50 Maria Valtorta, Poem of the Man-God, Volume 4, Centro Editoriale Valtortiano, © 1990, p. 214.

51 Taken from a letter sent to Caritas.

52 Elizabeth Rice Handford, Me? Obey Him?, Sword of the Lord Publishers, © 1994, p. 120.

53 Ibid., p. 23.

54 Ibid., pp. 24-25.

55 Ibid., pp. 23 & 25.

56 "Webster's New Collegiate Dictionary", G. & C. Merrim Company, © 1980.

57 "Inside the Vatican", August/September, 1995, p. 6.

58 Talk given by Ivan to pilgrims in Medjugorje, August, 1994.

59 Maria Valtorta, Poem of the Man-God, Volume 1, Centro Editoriale Valtortiano, © 1990, pp. 196-198.

60 Phone interview with "Focus On the Family's H.B. London.

61 Elizabeth Elliot, Let Me Be a Woman, Living Books, Tyndale House Publishers, © 1976.

62 Ibid.

Five "Must Do's" in Medjugorje

Apparition Mountain, Cross Mountain, the Visionaries, St. James Church, and the Caritas Mission House, these are the five "**must do's**" to have a complete Medjugorje pilgrimage. Throughout the years, pilgrims from every nation have made the Caritas of Birmingham Mission House in Medjugorje a part of their pilgrimage. Countless numbers have relayed to us that it is there, in the Mission House, where they came to understand more fully Our Lady's messages and plans for the world. It is why people, who have returned home from their pilgrimages, have told others going to Medjugorje to go to the Caritas Mission House, stating that the Caritas Mission House was a high point of their pilgrimage and a "**must do**" to make a pilgrimage to Medjugorje a complete and more profound experience.

Don't Miss a Visit to the Caritas Mission House

"After coming in the Caritas Mission House, I decided not to leave my husband and seek to bring prayer and healing into my family."
Pilgrim
Ireland

"I found peace and love in the Mission House."
Pilgrim
South Africa

"Following Caritas' mission for several years and observing their work in spreading Our Lady of Medjugorje's messages, it's no wonder to me as to how they became the largest Medjugorje Center in the world."
Pilgrim
Scotland

"The Mission House was the only meeting place in Medjugorje to learn more about and discuss the Messages."
Pilgrim
England

Look for the **St. Michael statue** and **"This is My Time" Signs**.
Caritas of Birmingham Mission House is operated by the Community of Caritas.
The Mother house is located at: **100 Our Lady Queen of Peace Drive**
Sterrett, Alabama 35147 USA

Mej.com *Extensive up-to-date information on Medjugorje as it happens.*

The Latest Major Medjugorje Book About God and What is About to Happen to Our Economy

After reading IT AIN'T GONNA HAPPEN!_{TM} people are...

✦ Realizing that their retirement is going away, and how they can act now to save it.

✦ Pulling every last dollar out of the banks.

✦ Realizing they are about to lose everything, and cashing out their entire 401K's, taking the penalty, and paying the taxes. Selling all their stocks and bonds, cashing out completely.

✦ Selling their dream homes, drastically downsizing, buying land, and taking other urgent bold steps now!

People are doing all of these things after just one read. WHY? When you read
IT AIN'T GONNA HAPPEN!TM
you will know why. The candle is about to burn out.

IT AIN'T GONNA HAPPEN!

A Return to Truth

By A Friend of Medjugorje

"It is when a people forget God that tyrants forge their chains. A vitiated state of morals, a corrupted public conscience, is incompatible with freedom. No free government, or the blessings of liberty, can be preserved to any people but by a firm adherence to justice, moderation, temperance, frugality, and virtue; and by a frequent recurrence to fundamental principles."

—Patrick Henry

★ Why have unbelievers, today, been allowed to get in positions to turn our laws upside down, destroying our Nation?

★ Why are the unbelievers in offensive positions, while we, Christians, find ourselves in defensive positions?

★ Why do individual States have to pass amendments to defend marriage?

★ Why can't we get Godly leaders in office?

★ Why have we lost authority over wickedness?

★ Why do the godless proudly parade their unmentionable and illicit lifestyles that cannot even be described in these writings, their abortions, their decadence, all the while imposing them forcibly upon society as the norm, flaunting in our faces that *"You cannot stop us!"*?

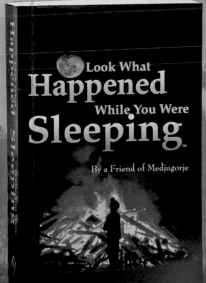

The #1 Most Popular Medjugorje Website in the World.

Medjugorje.com

✳ The most looked to site for direction on the messages given by Our Lady of Medjugorje

✳ Latest updates on Medjugorje

✳ Most extensive history of the apparitions: Beginning days, the 10 secrets, signs and miracles, etc.

✳ *RadioWAVE*™: Hosted by A Friend of Medjugorje, listened to by people all over the world.

✳ *mejList*: the Free Medjugorje newsletter

✳ Send your petition to Medjugorje and have it presented to Our Lady during the apparition

✳ Free downloads: audio, books and booklets

Dear Caritas,   June 5, 2011

"Thank you and many of God's blessings on a
purely soul-saving site!"

                    R.C.

Dear Caritas,   June 5, 2011

"I just wanted you to know how thankful we are for all you do
with Medjugorje.com. We found your site almost 1 year ago.
My wife and I have followed Our Lady's Messages ever since.
My life has changed. We just want to personally thank you for
loving Our Lady so very much."

                         T. & K.C.

Don't Miss a Visit to the Caritas Mission House

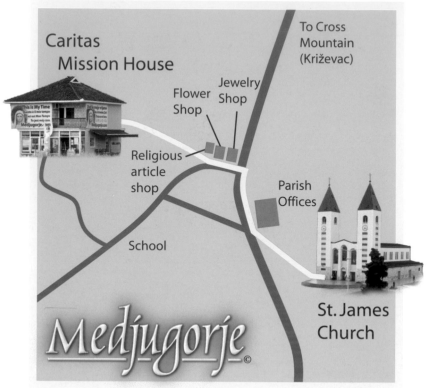

Located only two blocks from the church.
Facing the front of St. James Church from outside—exit the courtyard to the LEFT.
Walk past the Parish Offices to the main road and turn RIGHT.
Follow the sidewalk a brief distance to the next road and turn LEFT, crossing the road at the crosswalk. You will see a jewelry shop on the corner. The jewelry shop and a flower shop will be on your right as you pass it.
Follow STRAIGHT on the sidewalk a very short distance.
At the first road next to a religious article shop bear slightly RIGHT.
Follow this road past a row of Pansions until you reach the Caritas of Birmingham Mission House.
Look for the **St. Michael statue** and **"This is My Time" Signs**.

Caritas of Birmingham Mission House is operated by the Community of Caritas.
The Mother house is located at:　　**100 Our Lady Queen of Peace Drive Sterrett, Alabama 35147 USA**

Mej.com　*Fastest growing Medjugorje website in the world. Extensive up-to-date information on Medjugorje as it happens.*